AF437777

A Leap of Faith

Stephanie Swift

Published by Trellis Publishing, 2021.

This is a work of fiction. Similarities to real people, places, or events are entirely coincidental.

A LEAP OF FAITH

First edition. July 11, 2021.

Copyright © 2021 Stephanie Swift.

ISBN: 979-8224760695

Written by Stephanie Swift.

A LEAP OF FAITH

STEPHANIE SWIFT

Hope Miller laced her fingers together on top of her lap and did her best to empty her mind so she could focus on Bishop Abram's sermon.

It wasn't an easy task.

Sitting to her right was her mother and father, both of whom sat with rigid backs and facial expressions as hard and stern as the wooden pew they were seated on. To her left were her aunt Martha and uncle Seth, who both appeared comfortable and at ease, holding hands and smiling as they listened to the message. The two couples couldn't be more opposite if they tried, and she felt like neutral ground between them, which was disconcerting to say the least.

Hope cautiously looked over her right shoulder and smiled at Noah Wyse, her closest friend and ally. He sat a couple of pews behind them on the other side of the sanctuary with his six-year-old daughter, Ivy, who gave her a shy wave when she caught Hope looking their way. She wanted to wave back at her, but she knew if her mother or father caught her goofing off during the service she would never hear the end of it.

Noah gave her a sympathetic smile, and she turned her attention back to Bishop Abram before she made the mistake of smiling back at him and causing an uproar if one of the elders of the church caught her doing it. Even though she and Noah were just friends, it was highly frowned upon in their small Amish community for the unmarried men and women to cavort with each other unless they were promised to marry. It was ridiculous, really, but the last thing she wanted to do was cause a scene.

Hope sighed. If only things were simpler and less complicated. At twenty years old, she was one of the oldest from her generation who hadn't married, but that didn't bother her in the least. After growing up in a home with parents who shared a loveless marriage, a relationship was the furthest thing from her mind. Because of their strict faith, divorce was next to impossible, but there were many times during her youth when she wished her parents would go their separate ways. She couldn't imagine what brought the two of them together, unless it was an arranged courtship, because there was no way to picture them ever being in love.

Her aunt and uncle, on the other hand, were the epitome of love and devotion. You could see it in the way they looked at each other that their love was real. When Hope made the decision to leave home three years prior and move in with her aunt and uncle to help with her quilting business, the relief she felt was overwhelming. Gone were the days stepping on egg shells around her parents and living in a home that was so cold she could feel it in her bones. With Hope being their only child, she could only imagine how depressing the atmosphere must be now that they were alone together, and the thought made her heart ache.

No, she would never get married. Not if it meant she would lose a piece of herself and spend the rest of her days wishing for her freedom. No man was worth that.

Her mother nudged her side, startling her and making her jump. She hadn't realized she'd drifted off into her own little world, but the service was nearly over and every head in the room was bowed as Bishop Abram said his closing prayer. Hope shut her eyes as her cheeks burned hot from embarrassment. As soon as the Bishop said "amen", and everyone started for the door, her mother was on her case.

"Honestly, Hope...do you ever stop daydreaming?" she muttered.

Hope took a deep breath to keep from saying something she regretted. "I'm sorry, mother."

As they stood in line for the door, she glanced around the room in search of Noah and Ivy, but didn't find them. Hope peered through one of the church windows to see if they had already left the church, and she spotted them near a grove of trees with Victoria Kaufmann, a young widow from their area. While Noah and Victoria talked, Ivy played close by on a tire swing hanging from an old oak tree.

The two of them were deep in conversation about something, and when Victoria reached out and touched Noah's arm, Hope's temper bristled in response, which caught her off guard. *What was that about?* she wondered. She and Noah had never been romantically involved, and it wasn't the first time a single woman had flirted with Noah since his wife, Maria, passed away not long after Ivy was born.

"Are you alright?"

Hope looked behind her at her aunt Sadie, who was eyeing her skeptically. "*Yah*. Why do you ask?"

Sadie shrugged and smiled. "You just seemed puzzled for some reason."

Puzzled was putting it lightly, but Hope shook her head to clear her thoughts and to keep from dwelling on it. She and Noah were just friends, and it was probably just her over-protectiveness getting the best of her anyway. She knew very well how desperate some of her single friends were when it came to marriage, and she didn't want to see Noah hurt. That was all. He and Ivy had been through enough.

When they finally made their way outside, Hope and her aunt and uncle followed her parents to their horse and carriage to see them off, and Hope forced herself not to look in Noah and Victoria's direction.

"Sister, we would love for you and William to join us for lunch."

Hope rolled her eyes heavenward. It was the same thing every Sunday, and it always ended the same way - with her parents refusing. She would never understand how her aunt Sadie could be so patient with them when they treated her so callously.

Her mother and father stopped walking and turned to look at them. Her lips were pursed and her roughly chiseled face was set in her usual sour expression. Her father's face held no expression whatsoever.

"*Denki*, Sadie, but I'm afraid we'll have to decline. Hope, may I speak to you in private?"

Hope inhaled sharply and glimpsed at her aunt Sadie, who appeared just as perplexed. It was odd for her mother to want to talk to her about anything, much less alone. When she grabbed Hope's elbow and roughly led her a few feet away, she held her breath, expecting the worst.

"When are you coming home?" her mother asked.

Hope furrowed a brow as she pulled away from her mother's grasp. "What do you mean? I don't plan on moving back home. We've already discussed this."

Her mother huffed and puffed as she crossed her arms haughtily over her chest. "You need to stop being a burden to your aunt and uncle."

Hope took a step back. Her mother was never one to mince words, but her accusation stung. She looked over at her aunt and uncle, who were unsuccessfully trying to pull her father into conversation.

"I'm not a burden to them. How can you say that?"

Her mother wouldn't be swayed. "You're an adult, and you can't live with them forever. It's time for you to grow up and find a husband while there's still time."

Hope blinked twice. "While there's still time? You mean, while I'm still young enough to snag one?"

She didn't want to be disrespectful, but this time her mother was close to crossing the line. There was a significant difference between being concerned and acting downright rude. She hated to consider that she might be right. Did her aunt Martha and uncle Seth really consider her a burden? They'd never said anything about her overstaying her welcome, but perhaps they were just being nice.

Hope felt her eyes sting with hot tears, but she blinked them back, refusing to let her mother see that she'd gotten under her skin. Fortunately, she turned and walked back to the group before Hope had the chance to say anything further, which was probably for the best. The last place she wanted to fight with her was in the church yard with the whole congregation listening in.

She cast a wayward glance in Noah's direction, but he was still busy talking to Victoria Kaufmann and oblivious to everything else. Ivy noticed her right away and gave her a big wave as she swung back and forth on the tire swing with a silly grin highlighting her beautiful little face. Hope waved back before resigning herself to return to her family.

* * * *

Noah leaned slightly to his left so he could peek over Victoria's shoulder, and he felt his blood boil when he saw Hope talking to her mother. Actually, her mother was doing most of the talking, and he could tell from the sullen look on her face that the woman wasn't happy...as usual.

"Noah? Is something wrong?"

Her turned his attention back to Victoria, feeling guilty that he'd let his thoughts roam elsewhere. Victoria was a sweet woman, and even though he had no interest in anything other than friendship, it was obvious she felt differently. It may have been a long time since he was with another woman, but he knew flirting when he saw it.

"I'm so sorry. What were you saying?" he asked.

Victoria touched his arm again, something he noticed she was doing quite frequently while they talked. Any other man may have enjoyed it, but he'd already been blessed with the love of his life, and he wouldn't risk his heart being broken again. Plus, there was his daughter to think about, and he was far more concerned with her well-being than anything else.

"I asked if you were planning on attending the charity auction this Saturday. I'll be donating a picnic lunch."

So that was what she was getting at. It was all perfectly clear now. The auction was being held to raise money toward new books and other materials for their community schoolhouse, and it was tradition for the single women to make picnic lunches to be auctioned off among the single men. The winner would then share the lunch with the woman who donated it.

"*Yah*, I hope I can. It just depends on if I get my orders finished in time."

It wasn't a lie. Being the only blacksmith in the area, there was seldom a weekend that passed where he wasn't busy working overtime to finish orders. Not only did he have orders to complete for his neighbors, but several shop owners in nearby Lancaster were faithful customers too.

"Well, perhaps I'll see you there," she replied.

She gave him a shy smile before she turned and walked away, and Noah expelled a long breath. He stole a glance at Ivy as she played on the tire swing, and his heart swelled twice its size when she grinned back at him. She favored her mother so much it was hard not to look at her without feeling a deep pang in his chest.

He ached for the things she was missing out on not having her mother in her life. It wouldn't be long before she was a teenager, and even though he did his best to tend to her every need, there was a special bond a mother and daughter shared that he could never fill and he knew that. Ivy needed a woman in her life, and even though he missed the closeness and companionship a relationship provided, he just couldn't bear the thought of taking such a huge risk.

Noah caught sight of Hope and her aunt and uncle as he steered their horse and wagon out of the church yard and right on the main road, headed for home. Hope sat on the far right of the seat with her hands clasped together on her lap, staring off into the distance. Of all the women he knew, she was the only one he considered a close friend he could talk to and rely on. He'd bent her ear many times since Maria's passing, and she'd been there for Ivy more times than he could count.

If only they were on the same path. It wasn't as if he'd never considered the two of them as a couple, because he had many times, but Hope's parents made her jaded to the whole concept of love and marriage. Noah, on the other hand, knew the depths of love and what he stood to lose if he went down that road again, and it frightened him more than he cared to admit.

"Are you ready to go, daddy?"

Ivy appeared by his side, and when she placed her small hand in his, he forced the troubling thoughts from his mind and smiled at her. She needed him more than anyone else in his life now, and that was all that mattered. Everything else would have to wait.

* * * *

"I can't believe I'm doing this," Hope remarked.

She grimaced when she saw her friends standing in line at the auction, each of them appearing anxious as they waited to turn over their picnic baskets to Bishop Abram, who was serving as the auctioneer for the event. They were all clothed in what looked like brand-new dresses and bonnets, and they looked excited - giddy even.

"Oh, stop. It's all for a worthy cause. Did I ever tell you this is how your uncle Seth and I met?'

Hope looked beside her at her aunt Sadie, and she attempted a smile but failed miserably. If it hadn't been for her aunt's incessant nagging, she never would have agreed to taking part in such a silly tradition, but she'd come too far to back out now.

"Just look at those single men over there staring at you. I think they're memorizing what your basket looks like so they can bid on it."

Her aunt giggled as she said it, but when Hope saw the gentlemen she was referring to, her heart sank. There was Gabriel, one of the most conceited men in town, who thought he was God's gift to women, and there was Amos, a man three years younger than her who was at least a foot shorter than her too.

There were several other men in the group, but she didn't know most of them. She noticed Noah standing a few feet away, but she doubted he would take part in any of the festivities since he never had before. She'd managed to get out of it over the past four years, but her aunt had such a vise-like grip on her arm, she knew running wouldn't be an option this time around.

"Aunt Sadie, can I ask you something? I want you to be completely honest with me too."

Her aunt gave her a curious look before nodding.

"Am I a burden to you and uncle Seth?"

Her aunt tightened her grip and turned her around so they were face-to-face. Hope could tell by the look in her eyes that her question upset her.

"Of course not. You've never been a burden to us. Why would you even ask such a thing? Has my sister been filling your head with nonsense again?"

Hope smiled. Her aunt Sadie could always sense when something was bothering her, especially when it had to do with her mother. The two women were like night and day and had supposedly never gotten along during their childhood. As adults they merely tolerated each other, but it wasn't as if her aunt didn't try to build a relationship between the two of them. It was her mother who refused to budge.

"We love having you with us, and there's no way I could run my quilting business without you. You've been a Godsend, and don't you dare let your mother tell you any different. Now...get over there and get in line."

She gave her a little push and Hope had no choice but to do as she said. She made her way to the end of the line, literally dragging her feet with every step. If someone like Gabriel or Amos won her basket it would be the longest picnic lunch of her life. Hopefully, someone she could at least put up with for an hour or so would bid on her basket and win.

When Hope inched her way to the front of the line and handed over her basket to Bishop Abram, he looked surprised to see her. "I'm glad you're participating this year, Hope."

She prayed her feelings weren't painfully obvious on her face because she hated to disappoint him. Not trusting herself to speak, she simply smiled at him before making her way back to her aunt Sadie.

There were several other fundraising festivities taking place, and since the auction wasn't scheduled for at least another hour, the two of them walked around admiring the assorted pies, cookies, and other goods for sale. Hope tried not to dwell on the upcoming auction and have fun, especially since social gatherings were far and few between in her little community.

"Looks like Noah will have his hands full deciding who he's going to have lunch with," Sadie said.

Hope followed her gaze to the makeshift stage where the auction was going to be held. Noah stood off to the side of the stage, where he was flanked by three women – Victoria and two other women she didn't recognize. All four of them were talking and laughing, and the women's intentions were obvious by the way they batted their eyelashes at him and stood so close to him she wondered how he could breathe.

"It looks that way," she replied.

For reasons she couldn't explain, seeing the women fawn over him made her uneasy. The thought that he might be interested in one of them brought with it the realization that although they were good friends, it probably wouldn't always be that way, especially if he remarried. After all, what woman would put up with her husband having a close friendship with another woman, no matter how innocent it might be?

"Something troubling you?"

She turned to her aunt, who was eyeing her with an amused look on her face.

"No. Why do you ask?"

Her aunt put her hands on her hips and laughed. "Really, Hope? I have a tough time believing you don't feel a tad bit jealous seeing those women flirt with Noah. You had this same look on your face at church when you saw him talking to Victoria."

Hope's jaw slacked. That was crazy. Why in the world would she be jealous? They were just friends and nothing more. He'd mentioned many times how he wasn't interested in dating again, and...well, there was no way she would risk becoming as unhappy as her mother.

Before she could redeem herself, Bishop Abram was taking the stage and ushering everyone to sit down. Several of the pews from the church had been brought outside for the auction and as Hope and Sadie sat down on the middle row, she noticed Noah making his way to the back, were he stood behind the last pew. He waved at her when he caught her staring at him, and Hope waved back quickly and turned around to face the front, hoping he didn't see her cheeks burning red from embarrassment.

As soon as everyone was seated, Bishop Abram made his way to the podium and the table beside it that was littered with more baskets than she could count. She'd considered the number of single women donating to the auction, but she'd forgotten about the handful of widows, young and old, who might be participating – including Victoria Kaufmann.

Hope searched for her in the crowd and found her sitting near the front. When Victoria turned around in her seat, there was no denying her gaze was centered on Noah as a huge smile spread across her face. Even though Hope wanted to look at him to see what his reaction was, she forced herself not to, especially since her aunt Sadie was watching her every move.

Bishop Abram welcomed everyone to the auction before picking up the first basket – a large red wicker basket that he noted was loaded to the brim with homemade goodies like chicken and dumplings and blackberry cobbler. The bidding started at five dollars, and it didn't take long for the price to climb as several men placed their bids. It eventually sold for forty dollars to an older gentleman named Aaron, who'd been a widower for many years.

When Hope saw Clara, a middle-aged widow, pick up the basket and make her way over to Aaron and sit down, she wondered if she was the only one who detected the sly grin that passed between the two of them. She had to admit it was adorable, and part of her was kind of envious of them too.

The auction continued for at least an hour before Bishop Abram finally picked up Hope's basket. There were only three remaining, and Victoria was also waiting for hers to be called. She noticed Noah hadn't placed a bid on anything, which meant he was probably waiting on Victoria, and that bothered her more than it probably should have. Amos had, thankfully, already bid on and won a basket, so he was out of the bidding, but Gabriel hadn't, and that made her very nervous, especially when he turned and looked her way. The wink he gave her made her nauseous, and she considered running for the hills, but her aunt Sadie wouldn't hear of it.

"The winner of this basket will be treated to a fine lunch, complete with fried chicken, fresh corn on the cob, biscuits, pecan pie, and lemonade. Let's start the bidding at five dollars," Bishop Abram said.

Just as she feared, Gabriel waved his hand in the air.

"Five dollars!" Bishop Abram yelled. "Can I get ten dollars?"

A man she didn't know took the bid, but Gabriel trumped him by bidding twenty dollars. Hope started feeling sick to her stomach. *This couldn't be happening.* The two men kept going back and forth for what seemed like forever, and she could tell that Gabriel was getting annoyed.

"Who is that man?" Hope whispered, pointing to the other bidder. "I don't recognize him."

"He just moved here about a month ago," Sadie replied. "He bought the Troyer's old dairy farm."

Hope sighed. It was bad enough that she might be forced into having lunch with someone as obnoxious as Gabriel, but trying to find something to talk about with a stranger wasn't a fun option either.

"Sixty dollars!" Bishop Abram called.

Gabriel once again raised his hand, and when the Bishop asked for sixty-five, the other gentleman didn't make a move and neither did anyone else. It was the highest bid of the auction so far, which probably should have made her happy, but not under the current circumstances. Gabriel looked her way and the smug grin on his face made her stomach twist into knots.

"Sixty dollars going once, going twice..."

"One hundred dollars!"

Hope inhaled sharply, as did most of the crowd, when someone's voice boomed from the back row. She felt her heart catch in her throat. That wasn't just any voice. She would know it anywhere. Turning slowly in her seat, Hope saw Noah with his hand held high in the air. A hush fell over the crowd, and no one said anything for the longest time, including Bishop Abram, who appeared more stunned than anyone.

When he finally found his tongue again, he called for a higher bid, but no one made a motion to accept it. She glanced at Gabriel, who sat with his arms crossed over his chest and a scowl on his face.

"One hundred dollars! Going once, going twice...SOLD to Mr. Noah Wyse!"

Everyone clapped, and Bishop Abram held out her basket so she could come get it, but she felt glued to the seat. It took her aunt Sadie's prompting – or rather, *pushing* – to make her move, and when she retrieved the basket and turned to walk back, she didn't miss the look of contempt on Victoria Kaufmann's face.

Hope made her way to the back of the crowd and stood beside Noah as Bishop Abram picked up another basket she recognized as Victoria's. She wanted to say something to Noah, but she felt shy for some strange reason and so she stood beside him and waited for the auction to end. To say she was grateful Gabriel didn't win her basket would be an understatement, but Victoria wasn't so lucky. When he placed the highest bid on her basket, there was no denying the disapproving look on her face as she grabbed the basket from Bishop Abram's hands and sat down beside Gabriel on the front pew.

When the auction finally ended, Noah started walking in the direction of her aunt Sadie, which both intrigued and worried her as she followed him. When they approached, her aunt gave her another sly smile, but she rolled her eyes heavenward and chose to ignore it.

"Mrs. Sadie, do you mind if I take Hope home this afternoon?"

His question surprised her, but it didn't seem to faze her aunt, who agreed with more enthusiasm than she expected. When Sadie said goodbye and turned to leave, she didn't miss the little bounce in her step, and she knew without a shadow of a doubt that she would never hear the end of her aunt's gloating as soon as she returned home.

"So, where should we have our picnic?" Noah asked, after turning in his money to Bishop Abram.

Hope looked around the open space surrounding them and pointed to a large pine tree several yards away, which would help shade them from the blinding sun – and, more importantly, keep them far away from Victoria and Gabriel, who were heading in the opposite direction. Once they were settled on the blanket Hope had stowed away inside the basket, the two of them began unpacking the food.

"Noah, you really didn't have to do this. Not that I don't appreciate it, because I do, and I know the kids at the school will too when they get their new books."

Her comment made him smile.

"Oh, that reminds me, where is Ivy?" she asked.

Noah removed the aluminum foil from the plate of fried chicken and set it down between them while Hope poured two glasses of lemonade.

"She's spending the weekend with my parents. She's been begging me to stay with them for weeks now, and I finally gave in, but I didn't want to. The house is too quiet and empty when she's not there."

The tone of his voice made her heart ache, and Hope quickly changed the subject.

"I think Victoria was upset you didn't bid on her basket."

Noah chuckled. "She isn't my type. Besides, Ivy made me promise not to bid on anyone's basket except yours."

Hope almost choked on her lemonade, and she took a moment before she trusted herself to speak.

"That was very sweet of her, but I feel bad you spent so much money. I know how hard you work for it."

When he reached over and touched her hand, it felt...different. Sure, he'd accidentally brushed his hand against her skin many times over the years, but this time the warmth of his touch made her tremble, which had never happened before.

"Don't feel bad. I wanted to do it, and I had planned on doing it long before Ivy mentioned it."

Once their plates were full and Noah said grace over the food, they both started eating, and she was happy to see how much he enjoyed it, especially since she'd spent all morning cooking. They talked and laughed while they ate, and they were still sitting beneath the pine tree long after they finished their meal and the others had gathered their belongings and left for home.

Hope packed the basket and moved it out of the way as Noah stretched out on the blanket on his back and laced his fingers together over his stomach. She followed suit, being careful not to lay too close to him. The last thing she needed was for someone passing by on the main road to see them and get the wrong idea.

She sighed contentedly as she looked up at the pine tree and watched the branches sway with the wind. It was certainly a beautiful day God had blessed them with.

"Hope, can I ask you something? It's kind of personal."

She swallowed past the lump in her throat. "Of course."

When he turned over and propped his body up on his elbow so he could face her, she was suddenly very aware of how close they were. Several different emotions converged on her at once – fear, excitement, anxiety...even longing. She kept her eyes focused on the branches above her to keep from looking at him, worried that her face might betray what her mind and body were struggling with.

"Do you still not believe in love?" he asked.

Surprised by his question, Hope didn't know how to answer at first. "I've never said I didn't believe in it."

He looked at her as if she'd just made a funny comment. "Hope, come on. I know you better than anyone, and you've always made it perfectly clear that you don't want a relationship because of your parents."

She couldn't deny it, but the way he said it made her cringe. Were her feelings that transparent to everyone else she knew?

"Why does it matter so much to you what I believe?"

He sat up and rested his arms on top of his knees. He didn't answer her right away, and he avoided her gaze, but she didn't push him.

"I'm afraid your parents have poisoned your mind, and that matters to me more than you know."

Hope sat up and touched his arm, causing him to flinch in response. "Why?"

When he looked at her, there was something behind his gaze she couldn't quite grasp. Turmoil, maybe? Sadness? She didn't know, but it troubled her nonetheless. They'd had several personal conversations throughout their friendship, but this one was turning into something different...something deeper.

"When Maria died, I thought I would never be able to love again. I closed myself off to the possibility, but lately something's changed. I want that closeness in my life again. I miss it."

A twinge of jealousy caught her off guard and left her momentarily speechless. "I...I think that's wonderful, Noah. You deserve to be happy."

He solemnly shook his head as he peered ahead of him into the distance. "But the one person I feel I could have that with doesn't feel the same way, and I'm afraid there's nothing I can do to change her mind."

The way he stared at her, there was no denying who he was referring to, and the realization shocked her. She wanted to say something, but her tongue felt glued to the top of her mouth. He watched her and waited for a reaction, and all she could think of to do was run.

"We should go," she said.

Hope stood and started gathering her things, but Noah grabbed her arm to stop her. "Hope, please talk to me."

What could she say that wouldn't hurt his feelings and risk her losing his friendship? She honestly didn't know how she felt. Her heart and mind were jumbled with a thousand different emotions and none of them made sense. All she knew for certain was that she wanted to leave.

When Hope pulled free of his grasp and picked up her picnic basket, he hurriedly wadded up the blanket and followed her.

* * * *

Neither of them spoke on the ride to her house, but when Noah pulled up on the reins and brought the horse and wagon to a stop in her driveway, he quickly put his arms around her waist to keep her still before she tried to get away from him.

"Noah, please..." she whispered.

He felt her body tremble, and he wasn't sure if it was from the chill in the air or his touch, but he hoped with his whole heart it was the latter.

"No," he replied. "Not until you hear me out."

His heartrate escalated as the heat from her body sent an electric current coursing through his veins. She nodded in agreement, and he knew he should let her go, but it took every ounce of strength in him to release her.

"If it's your aunt and uncle you're worried about. I've already talked to them both, and they were very happy when I asked them if I could court you."

Hope's jaw slacked, and he instantly regretted not approaching the conversation in a gentler manner.

"You *what?*" she asked, her eyes wide and expressive.

Noah put a hand up to stop her before she flew into a tirade. "I promise I wasn't trying to do anything sneaky behind your back, but I'm determined to make you see that this...*us*...would work. You've just got to have a little faith in love, Hope. Your parents might be unhappy, but that doesn't mean you're destined to be unhappy too. I would never do anything to hurt you. You should already know that about me."

She appeared to be on the verge of crying, and he felt like kicking himself. Nothing was going as he planned, but he couldn't stop now. If he didn't get his point across before it was too late, he knew he risked losing her forever – even as a friend.

Noah gently touched her cheek and let his fingertips slide over her jaw to her lips. "I'm going to kiss you now," he murmured, softly. "Afterwards, if you can honestly tell me you felt nothing at all, then I promise I will let this go, and we'll never speak of it again."

Her eyes widened and she looked terrified, but he noticed she didn't shy away from his touch or try to stop him either. "Noah, no...I've never..."

He smiled as he tenderly cradled her head in his hands, "I know. You've just got to trust me."

When he leaned in close and pressed his lips against her own, he could tell right away how nervous she was by the way her lips quivered, but the effect she had on him was undeniable. His body burned hot with desire, and he felt the insatiable urge to take her in his arms, but he also didn't want to frighten her.

They separated for a moment, but he didn't let go. When she opened her eyes, he hoped he wasn't imagining things and that there was in fact a glimmer of want in her gaze. He didn't have to wonder long as she clutched the front of his shirt and pulled him to her. This time when their lips met there was no hesitation. She kissed him with a longing he hadn't felt in a very long time, and as their kiss deepened, she moaned softly into his mouth and gripped him tighter. When they managed to let go, they were both breathless.

"Does this mean you'll give us a chance?" he asked.

She didn't answer him right away, which worried him, but then he caught her smiling and his fears vanished. "It means I want to take this one day at a time. No rushing. If that's okay with you."

He nodded in agreement, and when she laid her head on his shoulder, he felt a renewed sense of hope that had been lost for many years. God was finally filling in the missing pieces of his life, and he looked forward to what He might have in store for him and Hope...and Ivy too.

Noah pulled her into his embrace and kissed her forehead.

"If you're by my side, that's all that matters to me," he replied.

And it was the truth. As long as they were together, everything seemed possible. Together they could face anything – and he was more than ready for the journey.

AN AMISH HOMECOMING

20

STEPHANIE SWIFT

David Montgomery walked the aisles of Alexander Mercantile & Grocery, shuffling about aimlessly while country music streamed from the overhead speakers. He'd picked up several items and given them the once-over before putting them back on the shelves with a dissatisfied grunt. If he were visiting a hardware store or lumber yard, this shopping trip would be a breeze, but trying to decide which brand of flour to buy for his mother's chicken pot pie recipe? He didn't have a clue.

He closed his eyes and groaned again. There was only one logical way to choose, but before he could eenie-meenie-miney-moe his way through it, he heard the soft sound of laughter from someone close by. David turned to find a young woman dressed in Amish clothing standing a few feet away, sorting through a shelf lined with oils and spices.

Peeking from beneath her white bonnet was a head full of long red hair, which was gathered at the nape of her neck with a blue ribbon. The bright red shade was a shocking contrast to her milky complexion and light blue eyes and gave her the appearance of a porcelain doll. The beautiful resemblance left him momentarily speechless, and when she walked over and picked up a small bag of flour and put it in his cart, he forced himself to stop gawking at her like a smitten teenager.

"If you're shopping for Miss Rosemary, you better get this brand or she'll tan your hide."

The mention of his mother's name brought him back to reality. It shouldn't have surprised him, given that there was only one Amish community in the vicinity – the same one his mother belonged to – and everyone knew each other by name.

"I apologize for the intrusion. I live a couple of houses down from Miss Rosemary," she said. "I'm Faith Somers."

She held out her hand, and David cleared his throat as he shook her hand and forced a smile. He noticed right away how soft and smooth her skin was, but her handshake was unusually firm and a lot like most of the men he'd met, which caught him off guard.

"David Montgomery. It's nice meeting you."

She nodded. "I recognized you from your photo. Miss Rosemary brags on you all the time."

David's thoughts flashed to the framed pictures of him his mother kept in her living room, and he felt his cheeks heat. They ranged from ages one to eighteen, and each year was more embarrassing than the one before.

"Well, I'll let you get back to your shopping. Have a blessed day, Mr. Montgomery!"

Before he had the chance to reply, she brushed past him and continued down the aisle without another glance in his direction. When she turned the corner and disappeared, David furrowed a brow. *Mr. Montgomery*? He hadn't heard that endearment since Bishop Luke presided over his father's funeral two years prior. Just how old did Faith Somers think he was?

David gathered the remaining items on his mother's shopping list and made his way to the checkout counter. He'd been in Dayton only three days, and he'd already talked to more people from the small Amish village than he could ever recall from the short time he lived there. So much for staying under the radar.

As an elderly gentleman scanned his groceries, David's gaze went to the large bulletin board on the wall behind the counter where several classified ads were posted. One in particular, with the headline CARPENTER NEEDED, caught his attention. The flyer's edges were tattered and worn, and the paper was faded, giving him the impression it had been on the board for quite some time.

"Excuse me, but do you happen to know the person who posted that ad?"

He pointed to the flyer in question, and when the cashier glanced at it, he shook his head. "Carson Andrews," he replied. "He was needing someone to help built a fence around his property, but that was a couple of months ago. Haven't seen him in here since then, so I don't know if he still needs the help or not."

When the man gave him his change and receipt, David scribbled the phone number from the flyer on the back of it. With any luck, the job would still be available. It wouldn't hurt to give it a shot.

"If you're looking for work, I might have something for you."

David turned toward the familiar voice and found Faith Somers standing behind him. As he folded the receipt and stuffed it inside the breast pocket of his shirt, she began unloading her shopping basket onto the counter. She stood so close he could almost count every one of her long, beautiful eyelashes.

David took a cautious step backward. "What did you have in mind?"

She smiled at him, and he could just barely make out the indention of dimples in her cheeks, which he had to admit was rather adorable.

"I inherited my grandfather's house when he passed away last year, and I've been meaning to hire someone to renovate the kitchen cabinets. Would you be interested?"

The thought of being in close quarters with a beauty like Faith intrigued him but also made him a little leery. After leaving the Amish way of life and starting over in a different city several miles away, the last thing he needed was someone or something tempting him to stay. Then again, for all he knew she might be married. If that was the case, then he was being ridiculous for no reason.

"Sounds good to me. When should I start?"

The cashier bagged her groceries and as Faith looped the handles over her right arm, he caught the elderly man watching them with an amused look on his face.

"Can you come by tomorrow morning, say around 9:00?"

He agreed, and as Faith made her way to the exit, he turned to look at the cashier, who was still smiling like a kid who'd been caught with his hand in a cookie jar.

"Do you know something I don't?" he asked.

The man looked down at the floor and chuckled before peering at David over his eyeglasses and giving him a look that teetered on the brink of sympathy. "All I'm going to say is good luck because I have a feeling you're going to need it."

With that, he turned and walked toward the back of the store. He never stopped laughing, and David couldn't help but wonder what he'd just gotten himself into.

He frowned. Perhaps he shouldn't have accepted the job so hastily, but unfortunately, there was no turning back now.

* * * *

The next morning, Faith put her hands on her hips and gave the kitchen faucet a resentful glare. She'd spent the past hour trying to replace the outdated equipment, but so far, the rusty nuts and bolts wouldn't budge. She gazed at her surroundings and let out a resigned sigh. Since the day she'd moved into her grandfather's old farmhouse, she'd been met with one obstacle after another. The ornery faucet shouldn't have come as much of a surprise, but it was more of an annoyance than anything. For once, she just wished something would go smoothly.

A loud knock on the front door startled Faith as she wiped the sweat from her brow and attempted to smooth the wrinkles on the front of her dress. She knew she probably looked a fright after her tug-of-war with the faucet, but at the moment she was too irritated to care what David Montgomery thought of her appearance.

Faith rolled her eyes heavenward. No, that wasn't the truth. After meeting him the day before, she hadn't been able to concentrate on anything else, so she actually cared a little bit too much what he might think of her.

She tucked a couple of wayward tendrils behind her ears and took a deep breath before opening the front door. David stood on the other side with a toolbox in one hand and a plate of cookies wrapped in plastic wrap in the other. It was odd seeing an English man standing on her front porch, and the sight of one in jeans and a t-shirt made her heart thump a little faster.

"Mom wouldn't let me leave the house without these, so I hope you like oatmeal cookies."

When he handed her the plate, their fingers grazed for a split second, but it was enough to make the tiny hairs on the back of her neck stand at attention. She stepped to the side to let him enter, and when he walked inside, she caught the faint scent of his cologne – a woodsy, masculine scent that tickled her senses and made her knees tremble.

"I love anything Miss Rosemary cooks," she replied. "Thank you."

As they stood facing each other in the tiny den, she was immediately struck by how tall and broad-shouldered he was. He looked larger than life, especially given their close proximity, and Faith tried in vain not to stare. When he suddenly closed the small gap between them and pressed his fingers against her right cheek, she thought for certain her heart would pound right out of her chest.

"You've got something on your cheek," he remarked. "Is that rust?"

He gently wiped the smudge away, and the heat from his touch made her light-headed as she cleared her throat and nodded.

"I've been trying to replace the kitchen faucet, and it hasn't been going very well."

She used his question as a chance to flee from the close quarters of the den and into a different room with more space to move around – and less room for touching. The kitchen was the largest room in the house, and as she motioned for him to follow her, she stayed two steps ahead of him and remained at arm's length as much as possible.

David placed his toolbox on the dining room table and looked around the room. "I see the problem," he replied with a grin. "These cabinets look like they rolled in with the Titanic."

His whole face lit up every time he smiled, and it was quite endearing and made the butterflies flip-flop inside her stomach.

"Everything in this house is ancient," she said. "I'm afraid it's going to take forever to renovate it the way I want to."

David opened his toolbox and took out a wrench, which he used to loosen the nuts and bolts on the kitchen faucet. After fighting with it for over an hour, Faith was dumbfounded when he had it completely taken apart in less than five minutes.

"There we go. Now, where is the new one?"

Faith shook her head as she placed the oatmeal cookies on a metal rack inside the refrigerator. "David, I appreciate the help, but you don't have to worry with that."

He shooed her comment away with a wave of his hand. "I don't mind. I bought an old ranch house that was in foreclosure when I moved away from here, so I know how time-consuming it can be. I'm happy to help."

Faith retrieved her shopping bag from Alexander Mercantile and pulled out the box containing the new faucet fixture. When she handed it over to David, he took to the task like a duck to water while she sat down at the dining room table and made mental notes for the other fixtures that needed replacing.

"Were you able to sell it?" she asked.

He stopped for a moment and gave her a quizzical look. "My house? Why would I do that?"

Faith was confused. From everything she'd been told, David had moved back permanently to care for his mother, but perhaps she'd misunderstood somehow.

"I'm sorry. I thought you were planning on staying here with Miss Rosemary."

David gave her a half-hearted smile, but he didn't reply right away, so she watched in silence as he tightened the bolts on the new fixture and made some other small adjustments before returning his wrench to the toolbox.

"I work in Franklin with the local fire department, and I just took a temporary leave of absence. I hope I'll be able to go back within the next two or three weeks."

For reasons she couldn't explain, his remark bothered her a lot more than she cared to admit. She wanted to say it was because she hated seeing Miss Rosemary living alone, but she knew that was only partly true. Maybe it was just her imagination, but she could have sworn there was a spark, an attraction – *something* – between the two of them, but perhaps it was one-sided. What did she know anyway? She couldn't even remember the last time a man flirted with her.

Faith stood and stuffed her hands inside her dress pockets. "I was hoping these cabinets could be painted white and the hinges and knobs replaced with something more modern. Do you think that's doable?"

He seemed taken aback by the sudden change in conversation, but she couldn't see wasting any more time on something that was unlikely to happen. If only she'd known his plans before offering him a job. With any luck, she wouldn't have to babysit him while he worked and she could stay busy doing her own thing – away from him.

David opened a couple of the cabinets and inspected the wood by running his fingertips along the grain. "It would take some sanding and a couple coats of primer, but I think they would look great painted."

Faith muddled through the next thirty minutes or so in a daze as they discussed color options and how long it would take to finish the job. She focused on other things in the room while they talked so she wouldn't be forced to concentrate on his piercing green eyes and the way his muscles flexed every time he moved.

When the details were sorted through, and David started working by removing the cabinet doors, she couldn't escape the house fast enough. Fortunately, she had chores to tend to outside that would keep her busy most of the day. As Faith closed the front door behind her and started the short trek to the barn, she whispered a silent plea for God to make the next two weeks go by as quickly as possible.

* * * *

David heard the commotion as soon as he walked outside, and he shook his head and laughed as he started for Faith's barn. The disgruntled groans and language that bordered on the obscene had become a common occurrence over the past two weeks, but no matter how hard he tried to help Faith with her chores, she always stubbornly refused.

David peeked his head inside the door, and he stifled another laugh as he watched her trying to milk one of the heifers. The animal was tied to a stall, and each time Faith leaned forward to grab onto her teats, the heifer would move just out of her reach. When Faith leaned over too far and fell sideways off the short wooden stool she was sitting on, David decided it was time to intervene before her temper got the best of her.

Before he could reach her, however, she kicked the stool several feet away and let out another frustrated groan that startled the heifer and rattled the tin roof.

"Whoa!" he exclaimed. "What was that about?"

He picked up the stool and brought it back to her, and he bit his tongue so he wouldn't laugh again when he discovered her sitting cross-legged on the ground with her arms staunchly crossed over her chest. She'd taken off her bonnet, and her lovely face was almost the same shade as her bright red hair. She looked like she could spit nails, and he approached her much like he did the bull in his mother's pasture – cautiously and with no sudden movements.

"I give up!" she yelled. "This cow hates me."

David set the stool down in front of her and sat down on it. "I seriously doubt that. I think she's just stubborn – kind of like someone else I know."

She flashed him a look of contempt, but he didn't waver, and they sat there in their own little battle of wills until Faith's shoulders slumped and she bowed her head.

"I don't know what I'm doing wrong. Nothing has gone right since I moved here last year. I'm starting to think I'm cursed or something."

Her voice was soft and sullen, and she looked so pitiful it made his heart ache. He wanted to console her somehow, but he had to fight the urge to take her in his arms.

"Faith, you're not cursed. I don't think you're giving yourself enough credit. I've seen how hard you work to keep this place running smoothly, and you're doing a great job. I'm sure your grandfather would be proud."

She looked up at him, and he caught a shimmer of tears in the corners of her eyes seconds before she wiped them away with her dress sleeve. If he'd learned anything in the past two weeks, it was that Faith Somers didn't want anyone seeing just how vulnerable she could be. He admired her tenacity, but sometimes he felt it did her more harm than good.

"I wish you would let me help you," he remarked.

It wasn't the first time he'd made such a request. He offered his help with the chores repeatedly, but she was adamant about doing everything herself. Faith was the most independent and stubborn woman he'd ever met, and it was admirable as much as it was irritating.

"David, I grew up with four brothers and no sisters, so I've spent most of my life trying to prove myself. My family has always treated me like a fragile wallflower, and sometimes I really believe that's why my grandfather willed this place to me. We were very close, and he knew how much I hated living in my brother's shadows."

It was the first time she'd opened up to him about something personal, and David was almost afraid to move or even breathe. He didn't want to ruin the moment, so he remained as quiet as a church mouse.

"When my family visits, it feels like they're watching and judging everything I do, so I have to stay on my toes all the time and make sure everything is perfect. It can be very tiring. I would love to have just one day to relax on my front porch with a cup of coffee and a good book."

David got off the stool and patted it with his hand. She sounded so downtrodden it was breaking his heart, and he was determined to help her in some way, even if she fought him kicking and screaming.

"What?" she asked.

She straightened her spine and was immediately on the defensive, as usual. Undeterred, David pat the stool again. "Come on. We're going to do this together, and you can either do it willingly, or I'll sit here and wait as long as I need to."

It didn't take as long as he expected it would, and with another one of her agitated groans, she sat down on the stool while he stood and took hold of the rope tied loosely around the heifer's neck. He coaxed the animal into position beside Faith before rubbing his hands over her head and down her neck.

"Now, I want you gently rub her stomach," he directed.

Faith crossed her arms over her chest again and gave him an incredulous look. "You can't be serious."

David tried to be as stern with her as he could. "You can attract more flies with honey than vinegar. Would you want someone with an attitude touching you?"

His question made her blush, and David immediately wished he'd worded the question differently. He didn't mean for it to come out sounding as flirty as it did, but she wasn't frowning anymore, so that was something. Faith placed her small hands against the heifer's stomach and moved them around in slow circles.

"She needs to feel like she can trust you, so take your time and don't rush," he whispered. "Rubbing her fur will help warm your hands too. They don't care for cold hands when it comes to milking."

He was trying to explain the technique as delicately as possible, so as not to offend her, but her cheeks reddened again. He felt like he should apologize, but before he had the opportunity, Faith started humming a soft tune and caught him off guard. He didn't recognize the song, but it was quite beautiful and seemed to lull the animal into submission.

David kept a firm grip on the rope while Faith placed a metal bucket under the heifer and began milking her. She continued humming throughout the entire process and the animal never flinched or tried to move away. He had to admit he was impressed. She stole a glance in his direction and when she flashed him a genuine smile, his heart thumped wildly inside his chest. When the bucket was full, she moved it out of the way and stood up slowly so as not to startle the heifer. She caressed the animal's back for several minutes, and when she stopped and took a step back, David felt like breaking into a raucous round of applause.

"That was amazing!" he exclaimed. "Well done!"

He noticed she stood a little straighter and jutted her chin out, like she was pleased with her accomplishment, and the change in her demeanor made him smile.

"Thank you, David. Your guidance made all the difference."

He could tell by the tone of her voice that it was a sincere compliment, and he swallowed past the lump in his throat before attempting to reply.

"You did the work. I'm proud of you."

An awkward silence followed, and David used the opportunity to untie the heifer and lead her to one of the empty stalls while Faith took the bucket and placed it on a table near the barn door. When he peeked over the stall, he caught her fretting with her dress and hair like she was trying to make herself presentable, and the sight made him smile.

David latched the gate and walked over to join her. "I finished installing the last of the hardware in the kitchen. Would you like to see it?"

For some strange reason, her attitude changed as soon as he asked. He didn't understand why, but her smile faded and she gave him a half-hearted nod instead of replying. He picked up the bucket of milk and followed her outside, but she kept her gaze locked on the large open field behind the house instead of speaking to him during the short walk.

When they made their way inside to the kitchen, he put the bucket on the dining room table and stood quietly by as she moved from one cabinet to the next, inspecting his work. She made the decision to go with a beige paint color instead of white, and he was glad she did because it gave the whole room a cozy and comfortable feel that was very inviting.

"Everything looks wonderful, David."

Her voice was low and solemn, and his curiously finally got the best of him. "Faith, did I say something wrong? You seem upset."

She turned to look at him, and he didn't know if it was real or simply for his own benefit, but she squared her shoulders and gave him a big smile. "I'm sorry. I guess I'm just tired," she replied. "I really appreciate your hard work over the past couple of weeks. It's beautiful."

She broke their gaze and looked at the cabinets again, and he still wasn't convinced she was telling the truth, but he didn't want to keep prying and risk making her angry. When he started gathering his supplies, she picked up his hammer beside the kitchen sink and placed it inside his toolbox.

"So, I guess you'll be heading back to Franklin soon?"

David shrugged. "I suppose so. Mom keeps hinting that she's ready for me to leave. I've taken care of everything on her to-do list, and I think she misses her peace and quiet."

He chuckled when he said it, but Faith either didn't think it was funny or she didn't hear a word he said, because her expression never changed. Their hands touched as he closed the toolbox, and the warmth of her skin sent an electric jolt to the tips of his toes. She glanced at him for a brief moment before turning and walking over to one of the kitchen drawers, where she removed a thick white envelope.

"Thank you so much for your help, David. I believe this is the amount we agreed on."

She handed him the envelope and stood by silently, as if waiting for him to count the money in front of her, but he put it in his back pocket instead. Honestly, he would have done the job for free if she'd let him. Being able to spend time with her was all the compensation he needed.

"Do you mind if I come by and see you before I leave?" he asked.

He expected her to say no, but he was pleasantly surprised when she said yes. He wanted more than anything to wrap his arms around her and pull her close, but instead he tenderly kissed her cheek. He hoped she might turn her head at the last second so he could kiss her lips, but she never moved a muscle.

Disappointed, David picked up his toolbox and left for home.

* * * *

Faith steered the tractor toward the barn and uttered a plea to the Lord for the ancient machine to make it there. For the past two hours she'd listened to it choke and sputter as she tried to get some work done in the field, and it lasted solely on a wing and a prayer. As she neared the barn, she caught sight of David traveling down the main road in Miss Rosemary's wagon, and she waved as he drew closer. Her heart raced uncontrollably, but it wasn't something she wasn't used to – especially when David was around.

She knew from the gossip filtering through the community that he was leaving for Franklin later that afternoon, and she hoped he was coming by to see her like he said he would. It was a moment she'd been looking forward to and dreading at the same time. She'd barely slept since the day he left after completing his work on the kitchen cabinets. She'd even contemplated finding some other job he could do that might keep him in town just a little while longer.

Faith managed to get the tractor a few feet from the barn before it started sputtering again, and she let out a yelp and covered her eyes when her line of vision was suddenly obscured by sparks shooting from the engine. She parked the tractor and killed the motor, but within a matter of seconds the engine was engulfed in flames.

Faith scrambled off the tractor and raced toward the well just as David came careening into her driveway. He'd barely brought the wagon to a complete stop before he was jumping over the side and rushing to help her. Everything happened so quickly she barely had time to catch her breath, but they were able to douse the fire with three buckets of water from the well before the flames reached the barn.

As Faith watched the last few puffs of smoke billow from the engine, she sat on the ground and pulled her knees toward her chest. She fought it valiantly, but her tears won in the end, and as they streamed down her cheeks she didn't try to stop them. It was all too much to handle, and she was so tired of the constant struggle. Maybe it was time to give up and let one of her brothers take over the farm. They hounded her about it constantly. Maybe this was a sign from God that she was meant to do something else.

David sat down beside her, but he didn't say anything, and for that she was grateful. She didn't want sympathetic words or to be coddled like a child. She wanted to be left alone to cry until she had nothing left. She wanted to drain every last teardrop from her body and soul and just get it over with once and for all.

They sat in silence for a long time, even after Faith stopped crying and settled down. When she glimpsed in his direction, she caught him looking at her with a big smile on his handsome face. He pulled a handkerchief from his pants pocket, and his amused expression never wavered.

"Feel better?" he asked.

If he was trying to annoy her, it was working, and as Faith jerked the handkerchief from his hand, she glared at him spitefully.

"Yes, as a matter of fact. I do feel better. I've seen the light, and I realize now that I'm not meant to do this, so I can finally move on with my life."

David scooted closer to her, and when there was barely an inch remaining between them, she held her breath expectantly.

"And here I was thinking you did this intentionally to try and keep me from leaving," he said, softly.

She knew he was joking, and she tried not to give in to it, but she couldn't help herself. Faith grinned as she playfully nudged his side. "Don't flatter yourself."

Her retort made him laugh out loud, and the deep sound of his laughter was like a healing balm to her rattled nerves.

"Look, I know it probably feels like the end of the world, but I promise it's not," he said. "This tractor is obviously very old, and I think it's served its purpose. Don't you?"

She glanced at the broken-down heap of metal and sighed as she thought back to the many times she'd ridden on the tractor with her grandfather while he worked in the field. He taught her how to drive it when she was thirteen years old, and it held a lot of wonderful memories from her childhood.

"The week before my grandfather passed away, I drove the tractor for him because he was too feeble to do it himself. I worked all day in the field, and I can still remember seeing the big smile on his face as he stood beside the fence and watched. He looked so proud."

David reached over and grabbed her hand, which caught her by surprise, but in a good way. Holding his hand felt like the most natural thing in the world. It felt *right*.

"I know I wasn't fortunate enough to have met him, but I have no doubt he was very proud of you," he replied. "And who knows, we might be able to repair the engine. Don't lose hope just yet."

Faith furrowed a brow. "Don't you mean *I* might be able to fix it? I don't think *we* would be able to accomplish much living in two separate towns."

He didn't answer immediately, but when he brought her hand to his lips and gently kissed her fingers, she felt a glimmer of hope stir deep inside her.

"I've been doing a lot of thinking the past few days, and I feel like this is where I belong. I know how strong-willed you are, and I admire that about you, but I want to be here for you, Faith. I was actually coming here to tell you that."

The small flicker of hope she felt began to diminish. "David, I appreciate you wanting to help, but you don't have to save me. I can manage the farm on my own."

He shook his head. "No, I think you misunderstood what I meant."

Before she could question him further, David leaned in close and pressed his lips to hers. It took only a few seconds, but she felt the impact from it through every nerve in her body. He kissed her again, but this one lasted much longer, and when he released her, she gripped his arm to remain upright.

"I don't want to just help you, Faith. I want us to be *together*. I'll understand if you want to take things slow, but please don't ask me to leave you because I don't think I have the strength to do that."

His voice was low and deep and his breath was hot against her skin. It was an intoxicating sensation that quickened her pulse and made her head swoon, and it was unlike anything she'd ever felt before.

"But what about your job?" she asked. "I would hate to see you give that up."

He smiled as she traced her jawline with his fingertips. "My boss is good friends with the fire captain here in Dayton. I'm sure he would put in a good word for me if I asked."

It took every ounce of strength she had, but Faith pulled away from him so she could focus on him without being distracted by his lips and the heat emanating from his body.

"But you left the faith, David."

He frowned as he sat up straight and looked up at the sky. She hated to bring it up, but if they were going to be together, they had to face the fact that it might not go as smoothly as they hoped.

"I've been thinking a lot about that too. I was young and foolish when I left, but now that I'm older and wiser I realize what I've been missing out on. I didn't think I would ever miss this way of life, but I do. I've felt more grounded and at peace since I've been here than I have in a very long time. I'm hoping the Bishop and elders will agree when I speak to them about it."

It made her heart soar hearing him profess his faith and his desire to return to it, especially since she understood the risk he was taking.

Faith placed her hand against his cheek and when he turned to face her, she pulled him close and pressed her lips firmly against his. It was a bold move, and one she'd never dreamed of taking before, but he seemed pleasantly surprised by the way he deepened their kiss. When they parted, they were both breathless.

"So...do you think I stand a chance with your family, or will your brothers give me the third degree and make me jump through hoops before they let me court you?"

Faith laughed. She hadn't considered what her family might think of their relationship, but she wasn't too concerned about it. If she'd learned anything since inheriting her grandfather's estate, it was that she was capable of making her own decisions and forging her own way in life. If they accepted David into the family, that would be wonderful, but if they refused, she still wouldn't let that deter their plans.

"Oh, I'm certain you can hold your own against my brothers, but I'll put my foot down if they give you any trouble. I know how to handle them."

David grinned as he wrapped his arms around her waist and carefully lowered her to the ground. "I don't doubt that at all."

As he softly kissed her cheeks, her nose, and her closed eyelids, Faith sighed contentedly while enjoying the whisper of his warm breath against her skin. After what felt like an eternity, God was finally bringing together the missing pieces of her life...and she couldn't wait to find out what He had in store for her future.

ABIGAIL'S DILEMMA

SAMANTHA COLLIER

Abigail Esh watched as the familiar hills and plains of her small Pennsylvania community fell into view. It had been a long buggy ride; they had been travelling for half a day.

She felt a small stab of excitement, at the thought of finally coming home. She had been staying with some friends of her family, who were English, for the past month. It was all part of her *rumspringa*. She had sampled many things in the big city, including going to art galleries and English restaurants. It had been enjoyable, of course, and she wouldn't change the experience for the world.

But she wanted to return to her community, and start life as a fully committed adult Amish. She was ready.

At last. Her family's farmhouse was in view.

As the buggy pulled up, her eyes took in every detail: the old ramshackle farmhouse, the outbuildings and hen house. Home.

The front door opened, and her mother was down the veranda steps. Her eyes were shining in excitement.

"Abigail! We thought you'd never get here," she remarked.

Abigail stepped down from the buggy, embracing her mother. It felt like she hadn't seen her in years.

"Mammi! It is so good to be home," she said. "Where is everybody?"

Mrs Esh smiled, a bit indulgently. "Daughter of mine, have you forgotten the routine already?" They walked up the steps to the house, arm in arm. "Your father and brothers are in the fields, of course. They will return for lunch, as is always the way. Your sisters are quilting, over at Mrs Troyer's, as they do every Tuesday."

Abigail flung herself onto the living room sofa as soon as they entered. "It was such a long trip, Mammi. I feel black and blue all over."

"How are the Carlisles?" Mrs Esh walked to the kitchen as she spoke, getting the coffee she had just made and two cups.

"Very good." Abigail sat up, rubbing her eyes. "They send their best wishes. It was a bit of a whirlwind, staying with them."

"I could imagine." Mrs Esh poured the coffee. "Come, have your coffee. It will revitalise you."

Abigail did as her mother requested, walking to the table.

Suddenly, she stopped. She could see the figure of a man at the front door – tall, dressed in the traditional Amish clothing. He had taken his hat off.

Who was he? She had never seen him before. And her eyes seemed to be unaccustomed to the Amish dress. She had been so used to seeing English clothes that it stood out to her. Well, she would get used to it, again, of course.

"Mammi." Abigail gestured toward the door. "Someone is here."

Mrs Esh rose, approaching the door. "Oh, it is only Nicholas! He is helping your father and brothers; he has been here about two weeks, from another county." She opened the door. "Nicholas! What can I do for you?"

The young man smiled shyly, looking from Mrs Esh to Abigail. "I am sorry to disturb you, Mrs Esh. Your husband sent me to tell you not to prepare lunch today, as we are planning to work through."

"Work through?" Mrs Esh frowned. "Stay for a moment, Nicholas. I will prepare something quickly for you all to eat, which you can take back with you. You can't all work from dawn to sundown without food in your bellies. Please, come in and sit down while I get something ready."

Nicholas hesitated, then walked through the door.

"Abigail," Mrs Esh said, "Could you please pour Nicholas a coffee, while I get the food ready."

"Of course, Mammi," said Abigail, glancing sideways at the handsome, shy young man. Who was he? Why was he working here?

"I'm Abigail," she said. "Please, sit down."

The young man did as he was told. Abigail poured him a coffee, then sat down beside him.

"How did you come to work with us?" she asked, taking a sip of her own drink.

"I was looking for some short term work," Nicholas replied, blushing slightly. "I am on my *rumspringa*, and wanted to experience life outside my community for a bit. My father knows yours, from many years ago, and got in contact." He paused, staring at her. "I'm sorry, but you are Abigail, who has been on your own *rumspringa*?"

"*Ja*," Abigail agreed. "I have only just returned, after staying with some English friends in the city."

"Did you have a good time?"

"I did," Abigail said. She looked at his hands gripping the coffee cup. Strong, and firm. "But I am happy to be home. The city life is not for me. The Lord has made that very clear."

"I am glad," he said, smiling at her. He had the bluest of eyes, the colour of the sky on a bright summer's day.

Mrs Esh came back in, carrying a paper bag filled with sandwiches. She handed it to Nicholas.

"Please, finish your coffee," she said, as he stood up.

"Thank you Mrs Esh, but I must return to work," he said. "And thank you for the food. I am sure we will all appreciate it."

He smiled at Abigail, ducking his head. Then he left.

Abigail stared after him, sipping her coffee thoughtfully.

What a handsome young man. And such polite manners.

It was good to be home, for a lot of reasons. And it seemed that there was one more good reason, although Abigail hadn't realised when she had walked through the door.

The day was full of surprises.

***

Now that she was home, it seemed like she had never left. It was funny, how life worked in that way.

She had already been home a week, and was back into the old routine. And the most exciting thing of all was that Nicholas, the shy young man who was helping her family with the harvest, had asked her out on a date.

She didn't know where they were going, as she excitedly got herself ready on Saturday night. But she knew that Nicholas would take her somewhere appropriate, as well as fun. They had just clicked, right from the moment that she had laid eyes on him at the front door.

But he was shy. She had found many reasons to go and disturb her family as they worked, sometimes bringing snacks or drinks. Her brothers would grin at her – they knew what she was up to. She didn't usually come to visit them so often. It had worked. Eventually, Nicholas had asked her out.

Now they sat in Stoll's restaurant in town, having just finished a hearty meal and laughing over a coffee.

Abigail had never been able to speak so easily to a boy. It was like they couldn't keep up with everything they wanted to say to each other. She felt a glow within her, as she looked at him.

They were just thinking of leaving when the door to the restaurant opened. Abigail turned to look automatically. Then wished she hadn't.

Oh, no. It was Christian Raber. She swivelled quickly in her seat, staring straight ahead. Her heart had started to thump uncomfortably. Maybe, if she was lucky, he hadn't seen her.

But her luck wasn't in. She heard his footsteps behind, approaching their table.

"Abigail." He wasn't smiling. "I didn't know that you were back in town."

She turned and looked at him, a bit fearfully. "Just a week," she said, quickly.

Nicholas was looking from Abigail to Christian. He seemed perplexed.

"I am Christian Raber," the man said, extending a hand toward Nicholas. "Abigail has lost her manners, it seems."

Nicholas took the man's hand, shaking it. He looked at Abigail. "And I am Nicholas Fisher."

She stood up, quickly. "We were just leaving, Christian," she said, walking toward the door. Nicholas' eyes widened, but he stood up, too, almost forgetting his hat on the table as he followed her. He had to go back to get it.

They exited, into the cold night.

Christian stood for a moment, staring after them.

His eyes were cold.

***

"What was that all about?" Nicholas had to run to catch up to Abigail.

She turned, stopping to catch her breath. "I'm sorry," she said. "I know that I appeared rude. But I didn't want to speak to him. He has this idea that he is in love with me, and I have given him no encouragement. Honestly." She blinked back tears, staring up at him.

"What does he do?" Nicholas was frowning, staring down at her.

"Oh, nothing much," said Abigail. She was appalled to find that her hands were shaking. Stop it, she told herself. "He is always polite. He just doesn't seem to understand that I am not interested."

She paused, shaking her head slightly. "I have told him enough times. But he doesn't seem to understand. When I next see him, at Church or Evening Sing or wherever, he asks me out again, as if he hasn't listened at all."

Nicholas assisted her up into the buggy. "I am sorry, Abigail. It is hard when someone doesn't listen to you."

"*Ja*," she agreed. She tried to shake the image of Christian, in the restaurant, out of her mind. She was on a date, with Nicholas. Handsome, caring Nicholas.

"Don't worry about it," she said. "I am sure he will realise, eventually."

They rode off, into the night.

They didn't look back. If they had, they might have seen the figure of Christian, standing in the dark street, staring after the buggy long after it had disappeared.

***

"He was in Stoll's Restaurant, Mamm."

Abigail was having a hot cocoa with her mother after the date. Nicholas had dropped her off half an hour ago.

Mrs Esh frowned. "Don't read anything into it, Abigail," she said. "It might have been just co-incidence. Who knows, maybe he needed to get something from Stoll's."

"At nine-thirty on a Saturday night?" Abigail was frowning, too. "No, I know him of old. He followed me there, I am sure of it."

"He never threatens you, does he?" Her mother looked at her over the brim of the mug.

"No." Abigail shook her head. "He is always polite. It's just a feeling I get. He always seems to be where I go, and he won't stop asking me to date him. I think after the first three negatives, he might get the message that I am simply not interested in him in that way. But he never does."

Mrs Esh stood up. "Time for bed, I think. I will talk to your father about this. We don't want to offend the Raber's, but Christian needs to know that he can't harass you. We will have to think it through carefully, though."

Abigail nodded, bringing her mug to the kitchen sink.

"I almost forgot." Her mother looked at her. "How was the date with Nicholas? We got so caught up talking about Christian."

Abigail smiled broadly. "It was lovely," she beamed. "I think that I really like him, Mamm. Do you think he likes me, too?"

Mrs Esh smiled, her eyes softening as she looked at her lovely daughter. "How could he not, my *lieb*?" she replied. "But I don't know how long he is staying for, Abigail. Your father said that he only needed help for a few weeks, and they are almost up. He lives in the next county."

"That's not so far," said Abigail. "We could write letters."

"So you could," agreed her mother. "But it really is time for bed now, Abigail. We have Church tomorrow, don't forget. And I have to be up very early to cook the goose for the lunch."

Abigail followed her mother up the stairs, preparing for bed. She glanced down at her Bible, thinking whether she should look at it tonight or not. It was very late. But she was still feeling jittery after her encounter with Christian, and felt like she needed some comfort.

Her head was drooping over the good book when she suddenly jolted fully awake. What had disturbed her?

She took her candle, and got out of the bed, walking to her window. She peered out into the darkness, but she could see nothing. She tried to shake the feeling of unease away from her. She was being silly. She should blow out the candle, and climb back into bed.

And yet she stayed, staring out the window. It was complete darkness; not even the moon was out tonight, and a thick blanket of clouds had covered up the stars.

She dropped the curtain, and climbed back into bed.

But the unease didn't leave her. Instead, it invaded her dreams...

She was running.

In motion, she suddenly stopped. She looked down at her feet, willing them to move. But it was like they were frozen in quicksand; the more she tried to dislodge them, the firmer they set. She twisted and turned, in a frantic bid to free herself.

He was coming. She knew he was right behind her.

Suddenly, the quicksand turned to ice. She attempted to run, again. But her feet were sliding over the ice. She stumbled, trying to regain her balance.

She heard a noise behind her, and turned quickly.

It was him. She couldn't see him in the shadows, but she knew.

The ice started cracking underneath her feet. She watched it zig-zag, broken veins across the white surface.

And then she was gone, underneath the ice, plunged into cold, cold water.

She stared up, and saw him looking down at her, coldly...

She sat up in bed, breathing heavily. She could feel sweat sliding down her neck.

This had to stop. She didn't know what Christian's intentions were, but he had to know how much he was scaring her. She didn't think that he would harm her, not really. But he was behaving oddly, and she couldn't deny anymore that it was starting to affect her.

She lay back down, drifting back to sleep. Think happy thoughts, she told herself.

The image of Nicholas filled her mind. His handsome face, concerned for her that night when she had told him about Christian. The way that he had helped her down from the buggy when they had arrived home, holding her hand tenderly so that she wouldn't slip. She had looked into his eyes, and seen kindness. His eyes shone with the purity of his soul.

Nicholas. Was she falling in love with him? But she hardly knew him. It had only been their first date, and they had chatted a handful of times before.

And soon he would leave. Return to his farm in the next county, away from her. His *rumspringa* over, just like hers was.

Would she see him again?

The image of Nicholas was the last thing that she remembered as sleep finally claimed her – this time for the whole night.

***

Abigail yawned, trying to stifle it with her hand discreetly.

It was the next day, and she was tired. It had been late before she had finally drifted off to sleep. She looked around at the familiar faces at the church service, but she hadn't seen him yet.

Nicholas. Her heart leapt as she said his name in her head, over and over.

Where could he be?

She tried to concentrate on the service, but her mind was drifting. Her mother had told her that Nicholas had attended their church service since he had been staying with them. And he himself had said that he would see her there. He had been looking forward to her mother's baked goose with apple and cider gravy for lunch, as well.

She surreptitiously scanned the congregation, again. But then she saw Christian Raber, staring at her from the back row. Shivers coursed through her; her skin crawled like it had been invaded by an army of ants.

She looked to the front, trying to concentrate on the service.

But her eyes, sickeningly, were drawn back to him.

He hadn't stopped staring. But now he added a small smile.

She refused to smile back. It would just encourage him. Silly, she chided herself. Even turning her head to look at him again he would perceive as encouragement.

He had always been an intense boy, ever since they had shared a seat in the one room classroom down the road. She could remember that he often would be alone, kicking a stone in the playground while groups around him played. And when he had friends, it would always be only one person, or two. Usually children who were a bit odd, like himself.

She had never been anything but polite to him, but she had drawn the line at friendship. She just couldn't stomach his intense stares. How he had perceived her politeness as anything other than that was beyond her. And yet he had. He had been asking her out for over six months now.

At first, she had been flattered, despite herself. But then it had got annoying. He simply wouldn't listen to her, when she said no. And then he started turning up everywhere that she went: a visit to the bakery, or when she was perusing stalls at the market. Anywhere.

It was one of the reasons she had gone so far away for *rumspringa*. Abigail wasn't much of a traveller, really. She probably would have stayed closer to home. But she had needed a break from his constant attention.

The service finally finished, and people started socialising. She went up to her mother.

"Where is Nicholas?" she whispered. "I haven't seen him today."

Mrs Esh looked at her. "I'm sorry, I forgot to tell you, Abigail," she said. "Nicholas received a note this morning, about something urgent. He needed to return home immediately. I'm not sure if he will be back, my *lieb*. He was due to finish work soon with us, anyway." She looked at her daughter. "Cheer up! You can still write to each other."

Abigail felt her heart sink. She shouldn't be so disappointed, of course. They had only had one date, and Nicholas had a life of his own, far away.

But she *was* disappointed. She couldn't deny it.

She was staring at the wall of the barn, lost in her own thoughts. She didn't see Christian approach until it was too late.

"Abigail." He bowed, slightly. His cold eyes were assessing her, as always. She often felt he looked at her like something strange he had just discovered on the sole of his shoe.

"Christian, I'm sorry, but now is not a good time," she said, quickly. Why was he always silent when he approached her? If she had some warning, she could have scurried away.

"I hear that the young man you went on a date with last night has left us," he continued, as if she hadn't spoken at all. "Very suddenly. Did you know that Frannie Glick knows him and his family? She was just telling me that he has a fiancée, back home."

Abigail gasped. She shook her head. "No, Christian, I am sure that you are mistaken," she replied. "Nicholas didn't mention anything to me about a fiancée. He is an honourable man."

"Is he?" Christian smiled, coldly. "How well do you really know him, Abigail?"

She frowned. She supposed it was true, to a degree. She had only known Nicholas a week, after all.

But she trusted her instincts. He was a good man, she knew it. He wouldn't have deliberately deceived her about having a fiancée.

"Well, I shall talk to him," she said, turning away. "I really must go, Christian. I have to help my mother with the lunch."

She walked away quickly, ducking amongst people. Hopefully he wouldn't follow her.

Was it true? He had said he had got the information from Frannie Glick. She looked around, but couldn't see her.

She frowned. Oh, well. Frannie would turn up, sooner or later. And then she would ask her, how she had come by this information that Nicholas had a fiancée.

As Christian claimed.

She felt the skin crawling on the back of her neck. She looked around, and, of course, he was staring at her. An upsurge of anger shot through her. Would he ever leave her alone?

***

"He did mention a girl he had been dating..." Mrs Esh frowned, squinting her eyes, trying to remember. "Or was it that they had dated in the past? I'm sorry, Abigail. I simply don't remember. But he never mentioned a fiancée, of that I am sure."

Abigail frowned, too. It wasn't the simple yes or no answer that she was wanting. This was very frustrating.

She didn't have a right to demand an answer of Nicholas. They had made no promises to each other; it had only been one date, after all. But she also felt that he did owe her an answer, because it simply wasn't done to be dating someone behind his fiancée's back, if he had one.

If it was true, she never would have agreed to go out with him. It was as simple as that.

Restless, Abigail stood up. "Do you need me for anything else, Mamm? If not, I might go to my room, study my bible for a while."

Mrs Esh looked at her. "Of course, Abigail," she said. "Just come down to help with supper, that's all I require."

Abigail left, bounding up the stairs.

Mrs Esh watched her go, shaking her head slightly.

Her daughter was in a state, and had been since Nicholas had left so suddenly the day before. Mrs Esh was worried about her. It was unlike Abigail. And what was this business with Christian Raber? Abigail hadn't mentioned it to her until after her date with Nicholas. If it was true, it wasn't good, and they should intervene on her behalf. But what if Abigail was just being fanciful? The Rabers were good friends of theirs. Mrs Esh didn't want to cause conflict without reason.

She frowned, pondering. No, they would do nothing, for now. If Abigail continued to be worried, well, they would do something then.

She sighed. It was hard, being young. Navigating your way into adulthood. She might mention some bible passages that Abigail should study, to try to ease her mind.

***

Abigail finished the letter, signing her name at the bottom thoughtfully.

She had been in two minds about whether to write to Nicholas, but she was so wound up she didn't know what else to do. Even if she didn't send the letter, it had felt good to get her thoughts and feelings out onto paper.

She read back over what she had written. She had tried to not be too intense, but still convey her wish to continue corresponding with him. She hadn't mentioned anything about him having a fiancée, except to implicitly imply that if he was seeing someone where he lived, she would stop communicating with him.

She put the letter in an envelope, and sealed it. She wasn't sure of his address; she would have to ask her mother if she knew it.

She left it on her desk, propped up against her lantern.

It was time to help her mother with supper.

***

Outside the farmhouse, Christian could see Abigail leave her desk. He saw the letter. He could guess who it was to. And he knew how to solve this, as well.

He often watched her. He had found a position, quite hidden. He would come over the back way to the house, through the fields, being careful to avoid her father and her brothers working.

He didn't think that he was doing anything wrong. He had, after all, explained to her that he wanted to take her out. It was his intention to make her his wife. She was hesitant, and had said no, but that didn't unduly concern him. His father had told him that girls sometimes said no when they meant yes. His own mother, apparently, had refused his father a few times before finally agreeing to date him.

She just needed a little bit of persuasion, that was all.

He frowned, thinking of when he had walked into the restaurant and seen her on a date. It simply would not do. No other man was allowed to date his Abigail.

It had been a stroke of luck that Nicholas Fisher's father had suddenly needed him back at home; as soon as he had heard that, he seized the opportunity. Frannie Glick was away on her *rumspringa*, and couldn't contradict his story about a fiancée. Frannie was a friend of his, anyway, and as soon as she was back he would contact her and persuade her to corroborate the story.

He smiled. It was all going to plan. He had to get rid of Nicholas once and for all, discredit him in Abigail's eyes. And then he would be there, to pick up the pieces.

She would finally see that he was the one for her.

***

The letter had been sent. Abigail waited for a response, but none came.

Inside, she fretted a little. It was all so strange. She had thought that she and Nicholas had a real connection. But he wasn't responding to her – did that mean that what Christian said was true? That Nicholas had a fiancée back home, and that she had been a diversion while he was away?

But as the days went by, and no letter came, Abigail had to admit it to herself. Nicholas didn't care.

Oh, well. She went about her chores as normal, and smiled and laughed when she was required to. She let no one see her sorrow. It would get better, in time. Of course, it would. They had only known each other a short time. It wasn't as if it was a deep wound.

She studied her bible. The classic passage from Ecclesiastes 3:4, about there being a time for sorrow as well as joy, comforted her. She knew that life couldn't be good, all the time. You could learn from sorrow, and had to accept that sometimes there was sorrow in life. As surely as the tides ebb and flow on the shore, sorrow and joy would come and go.

So Abigail kept telling herself, as the days drifted into weeks.

***

The women sat around the table, picking up their needles to commence their quilting bee.

Abigail picked up hers with a sigh. It had been three weeks, and she had not received a word from Nicholas. It was time to let it go, put it behind her. They had connected, but he had decided that it wasn't worth pursuing. Or, he did have a fiancée at home, and he had been merely dallying with her. Abigail preferred to think it was the former; she didn't want her last impression to be that he was a dishonourable man.

They heard another buggy pulling up outside the farmhouse. The women looked at each other.

"Are we expecting someone else?" Mrs Esh turned to the women.

Frannie Glick walked through the door, puffing slightly.

"Frannie!" Mrs Mueller put down her needle. "We weren't expecting you! Aren't you supposed to be on your *rumspringa*?"

"*Ja*," answered Frannie, smiling at the group. "I returned yesterday, a few days early. Mammi told me that you were meeting today, and I wanted to catch up with you all."

Frannie took her seat, and started answering questions about her *rumspringa*. She had been staying with cousins in Ohio, and had a wonderful time.

Abigail glanced at her as she worked. She was waiting for the break, so she could ask her about Nicholas. It probably didn't matter, anymore. But she wanted to know.

At last, the women started getting up. One went to the kitchen, to prepare coffee and snacks. Frannie rose, and walked to the window.

"Frannie," Abigail said, walking up to her. "It is nice to have you back. I was just interested to know. Christian Raber was telling me that you know Nicholas Fisher and his family."

"Who?" Frannie looked at her, a puzzled expression on her face. "I don't know any Nicholas Fisher, Abigail. I think you must be mistaken."

"Are you sure?" Abigail frowned. "Christian told me that you knew the family, and that Nicholas had a fiancée back where he lives."

Frannie continued to look at her, bewildered. "I have no idea what you are talking about, Abigail. The only Nicholas I know is Nicholas King, who we went to school with."

"I'm sorry," Abigail said. "I must have misheard him. Thank you, anyway."

She turned around, and walked out of the house. She needed to be alone, for a moment. She needed to think.

She sat down on a seat on the porch, thinking deeply.

Frannie didn't know the Fishers. She had never heard of Nicholas. Which meant one thing: Christian had lied to her. About Frannie knowing them, but also about Nicholas having a fiancée.

She felt herself go cold. This was getting serious.

Christian had always been an annoyance. But now, he was actively interfering in her life.

She didn't know what to do. Just that it had to stop, once and for all. He had no right, and she was going to make sure that he knew it.

***

Abigail dressed carefully for the meeting.

She had spoken to Mrs Raber, asking her could she come over for a visit. There was something she needed to discuss with her and her husband, urgently. She also requested that Christian be there for the meeting.

She didn't tell her mother. She knew that she would be concerned about making waves with the Rabers. It was something she was concerned about, too. But she also knew that it couldn't continue. Christian had to be stopped. And the best way of ensuring that was to enlist his parents. Abigail knew Christian. He was obedient to his parents, and his father ruled him with an iron fist.

And it was something that she felt must do, by herself. She had to stand up for herself, once and for all.

Mrs Raber opened the door, and led her to the kitchen table. Coffee and cakes were there, waiting.

"Oh, you shouldn't have gone to so much trouble," Abigail said. She was sweating, a little, and her hands when she took the coffee cup were shaking. She wasn't looking forward to this.

Mr Raber was already there, looking at her expectantly. And then Christian came into the room.

He didn't look happy. But he sat down at the table. Obviously, his parents had insisted.

"So." Mrs Raber looked at Abigail, expectantly. "What did you need to see us about so urgently, Abigail?"

Abigail cleared her throat. She must be strong, but she was very nervous. It could backfire on her, and the Rabers might evict her from their home, saying that she was lying.

How should she proceed?

"Thank you for seeing me," she stated. "I know you are all busy people. I needed to see you about Christian."

Christian looked at her, his face like thunder. She almost balked, but doggedly continued.

"As you know, Christian and I have known each other a long time," she said. "Since school. I have always liked him as a friend, but lately, Christian has been wanting to court me."

Mr Raber smiled. "Nothing wrong with that."

"No," Abigail continued. "There isn't. But I have told Christian many times that I am not interested in him that way, and he continues to pester me. He doesn't listen to my wishes."

Mrs Raber looked at Christian, anxiously. "Is this true, Christian? Have you been pestering Abigail, when she has clearly said no?"

"She wants to go out with me," Christian blurted. "I know she does! She just needs persuading. Isn't that so, Daed? You always told me that women often don't know their own minds, and need a firm hand."

Mr Raber frowned. "That is not what I meant, Christian. Yes, sometimes a girl takes a bit of wooing. But if a young woman has clearly said no to you, repeatedly, then you must do the honourable thing and accept her decision."

"But...but..." Christian shook his head, colouring. "I know that she loves me, deep down!"

Abigail looked at him, coldly. "That is wrong, Christian," she said. "I don't love you, and never will. I have no desire to hurt you, but you must accept what I say. I don't want to court you. I like you just as a friend." That was a little white lie. She didn't like Christian, at all. But she didn't want to completely destroy his confidence in himself.

"Abigail, your wishes will be respected," said Mr Raber, glaring at his son. "I will make sure of it. Christian will not bother you anymore."

"Thank you," breathed Abigail. She turned to Christian.

"I wish you well, Christian," she said. "I hope that you find the woman that you will marry, one who loves you. But she is not me. I hope we can still be friends. Will you shake my hand?"

She offered her hand across the table to him. He looked at it as if he might refuse, then he grudgingly shook it. Mrs Raber looked relieved.

"I must go," said Abigail, rising. "Thank you all so much for letting me speak, and taking me seriously. It means the world to me."

"God speed, Abigail," Mrs Raber replied. Mr Raber smiled at her.

It was over. Christian would not bother her, again. She knew the Rabers, and that they demanded complete obedience. Christian would not dare to defy them, now that they knew. She would have preferred that he realised by himself, but that might never happen.

She had to protect her life. He had already interfered in her budding relationship with Nicholas. She didn't want him to interfere for a minute longer.

***

Abigail was feeding the hens when a shadow fell across her.

Fear gripped her. Oh, no. It wasn't Christian back – was it?

She looked around. Then gasped. It wasn't Christian who stood there, but another tall man.

It was Nicholas!

She stood up, slowly. She couldn't quite believe that he was here.

He smiled at her, a bit tentatively. "Abigail," he said. "Your mother said that you would be here."

"Here I am," she replied, then could have kicked herself. Couldn't she think of anything better to say?

"Do you want to go inside?" He asked. "I need to talk to you."

She nodded, leading the way out of the hen house.

They sat at the kitchen table, staring awkwardly at each other.

"I thought…"

"I'm sorry…"

They laughed, as they realised they had both spoken at the same time.

"You go," said Nicholas, looking at her as if he had never seen her before in his life. It made her glow.

"I thought that you didn't want to see me again," Abigail said, biting her lip.

"I thought the same," Nicholas replied. "When you didn't answer my letter."

"What letter?" Abigail frowned. "I never received a letter from you. I wrote *you* a letter, which you never replied to!"

Nicholas shook his head, frowning. "I don't understand. I never received a letter from you. But I did send one."

Abigail stared at him, perplexed. Then understanding started to dawn on her face.

"It must have been Christian," she said. "I didn't realise he was going to that level. He must have been monitoring our mail box. Mamm leaves letters we want to send in there for Daed to collect and send when he gets to town."

"Christian?" Nicholas frowned. "That man who has been pestering you?" He paled, and stood up. "This is going too far. I will go around to his house, this minute!"

"Nicholas, sit down," Abigail said. "It's alright. I have spoken to his parents. He won't be bothering me anymore."

"Are you sure?" Nicholas sat down, slowly. "Because if he ever tries again, he will have me to answer to!" Abigail could see a vein throbbing in his temple. He was angry.

"So you care about me?" She looked at him, shyly.

"I do," he replied. "So much so, Abigail, that I travelled here today to speak to you, even though I thought you didn't answer my letter." He paused, looking like he didn't know what to say further.

"I care for you, too, Nicholas," she said, shyly. "Can we begin again? Like before Christian started interfering in our lives. He told me you had a fiancée, back home."

"He what?" Nicholas looked gobsmacked. "That is an outright lie! I would never have asked you out on a date if I had a fiancée. You didn't believe it, did you?"

"I tried not to," Abigail answered. "But when you didn't reply to my letter, I thought the worst. It was Christian, all along."

"We can begin again," Nicholas said, looking at her earnestly. "If you are willing?" He reached for her hand, across the table. "And God willing, of course."

"Nothing would please me more," Abigail replied. She took his hand. Happiness swelled up within her.

Christian was out of their lives. Nicholas cared for her.

The time for joy was upon them.

THE END

KAYLA

62

MONICA MARKS

It was Kayla's favorite time of year and when she woke that morning, she inhaled deeply, absorbing the nostalgic feeling which the onset of autumn brought along.

It is time for harvest and engagement announcements, she thought happily, swinging her long legs off the single mattress and scurrying to the window to stare into to endless farmland. The smallest frost had settled overnight but there was no cause for concern; the sunshine was fighting to warm the October day already and it was just past dawn. She tried to ignore the near exhaustion in her bones and stretched, willing herself to wake up.

I slept more than enough, she reasoned with her weary body. *There is no reason for me to be so tired.*

She told herself that the crisp fall air would invigorate her.

"Kayla!"

Her younger sister, Hannah threw open the door to her bedroom and folded her small arms across her chest.

"Haven't you dressed yet? It is almost seven o'clock!"

"Haven't you learned to knock yet? You are almost eight years old," Kayla replied haughtily. The sisters stared at each other before bursting into laughter.

"I am coming, Hannah," she assured the child. "There is time for breakfast and to walk to school."

Hannah smiled and Kayla clapped her hands.

"You lost another tooth!" she declared, rushing forward to examine her sister's mouth. "Let me see."

Hannah opened her mouth obligingly and the older sister patted her cheek.

"Go show *Daed* now," she instructed. "I will be along in a moment."

Hannah turned to leave Kayla, rushing down the steps toward the kitchen and Kayla hurried to change.

Hannah was not wrong; she had slept in again. It seemed to be happening with more frequency and Kayla had first believed the change of weather had been affecting her but suddenly she was not so certain.

I must eat better, she chided herself, slipping into a dark brown work dress and fastening an apron atop her skirt. *Autumn is not the time to waste time sleeping when Daed needs help with harvest and winter preparations. If you are so tired when the days are still long, what will you be like in two months?*

She padded across the threshold and into the corridor, trying to recall what needed to be done that morning. Canning needed to be started, the hay baled, pickling, jams...the list was endless as always and Kayla began to form a list in her mind in order of importance.

Slipping down the stairs, Kayla was suddenly overwhelmed by a wave of dizziness. She clutched the bannister, blood draining from her face as she tried to gather her bearings.

Oh Gotte, I do not have the luxury of being sick, she warned herself, willing a feeling of normalcy to come but in seconds, her legs had buckled and to her horror, Kayla tumbled down the remaining three steps onto the landing.

Not again! She thought, horrified, knowing that her family would witness her embarrassment this time. It was the third fainting spell she had experienced in two weeks but gratefully, her father and sister had not seen the others.

As spots of black and red danced before her eyes, she opened her mouth to moan but she began to lose consciousness as Hannah came running into the foyer, their father in tow.

The last thing she recalled before the world went dark was her small sister screaming.

When she woke, Jeremiah Roth stood praying over her, his eyes closed but even without reading the expression in his gentle blue irises, Kayla could see the concern in his face.

"*Daed*?" she called weakly, struggling to sit up against the bed. She realized she had been put back in her room, tucked in snugly among blankets.

"Oh, Kayla!" Jeremiah gasped, his lids flying open at the sound of her voice. "You must remain still. I have asked the Fishers to call for Dr. Imhoff."

"I am fine, *Daed*," Kayla protested. "It was nothing, I am sure. It happens sometimes."

"How many times?" Jeremiah demanded, his cornflower blue eyes wide with shock. "Why did you not tell me before?"

"It is no cause for alarm. Cancel the doctor!" Kayla groaned.

"Hush, *liebchen*," he insisted, pointing at the bed. "You will remain here until the doctor has seen you."

"We haven't time for this," Kayla insisted, attempting to rise again. "We have much to do."

"I am your father," Jeremiah growled with uncharacteristic sternness. "You will do as you are told. The harvest can wait."

Kayla settled back, blinking.

"All right, *Daed*," she relented. "I will wait but the Dr. Imhoff will tell you there is nothing wrong."

"I would rather hear it from him," Jeremiah replied. "He is the one with the medical degree after all."

He turned to the bedside and produced a glass of water.

"Drink this. I will wait downstairs Jonah."

"Where is Hannah?"

"Lydia Fisher has taken her to school. You mustn't worry, Kayla. All is tended to this morning. Your job is to rest."

He turned to leave the room before Kayla could form another argument, leaving her to stare at the ceiling is mild exasperation.

This is foolish, she thought but she dared not express her feelings aloud. She knew her father was concerned and she had no one to blame but herself.

I have been neglecting meals and sleeping poorly, she chided herself. *Now I have worried everyone.*

In minutes, she heard footfalls on the stairs and the door opened.

"*Guter mayire,* Kayla," Dr. Imhoff announced, smiling in his kindly way. "I understand you had a small fainting episode this morning."

Kayla stifled a sigh.

"It was nothing," she insisted.

"I will see about that," Jonah Imhoff replied lightly, opening his bag.

He checked her eyes and throat, running her temperature and pinching her skin to test for validity.

Then he turned to Jeremiah.

"We will talk outside," he told the patriarch, patting Kayla's face warmly.

"You should rest today, Kayla," he told her, closing his bag. Kayla chewed on her tongue to keep a thousand objections from erupting and watched helplessly as the men retreated into the hallway.

She strained her ears to listen, catching only a few words as she did.

"...tests...color...must be vigilant."

Their voices cut in and out but Kayla felt a prickle slide down her back as she understood the gist of their conversation.

He believes there is something wrong with me, she realized, concern floating through her for the first time since the incidents had begun. She tried to dismiss the feeling of worry but when her father returned to the bedroom, his eyes shone with something she had not seen in many years.

"Jonah is arranging for you to have tests done at Lancaster General Hospital," he told her gravely. Kayla swallowed quickly, realizing there was a lump in her throat.

"What does he believe is wrong, *Daed*?" she whispered and Jeremiah seemed to recognize his mistake, wiping the dismayed frown from his face.

"Nothing specific, *liebchen,*" he replied quickly. "It is merely a precaution. Do not fret; we will learn what ails you soon enough."

"*Daed,* I am certain it is - "

"You are not a doctor, Kayla. In the meanwhile, you will rest. I will see if Lydia can stay with you while I tend to the farm," he continued and Kayla heard no room for debate in his tone.

"*Daed,* you cannot tend the farm alone," she sighed. "You would better have Lydia help you."

Jeremiah stared at her for a long while as if he was looking directly through her.

"You are correct," he told her softly. "I must enlist help until you are better."

Without another word, he spun and walked from the bedroom, leaving Kayla to stare after him with her mouth agape in question.

The wagon drew near the farmhouse, Lydia Fisher leading the horse through the grey day. They were returning from Kayla's appointment at the hospital where she had undergone bloodwork for her ever increasing fainting and general fatigue.

"Would you like me to come with you, Kayla?" Lydia asked as she slid from the bench onto the dirt. Kayla stifled a sigh and shook her head, forcing a smile onto her lips. She was growing tired of being coddled by both her father and the neighbors, despite their good intentions.

"I feel fine," she fibbed. In reality, she wished to lay down but she dared not say anything to Lydia. The last thing she wished to do was cause more of a fuss.

"I will be by later this evening to fix supper for you," Lydia told her, picking up the reins. "Back to bed now."

Kayla did not answer but waved at the butcher's wife as she made her way from the Roth farm toward her own.

I will go mad if I have to spend one more minute in bed, Kayla thought glumly, turning toward the fields. She saw her father in the distance, reaping corn and she longed to run toward him but she did not. She would only interrupt him and take more time from his duties.

Duties I should be tending to also, she told herself, guilt wracking her body.

The doctor at the hospital had been candid with her assessment, citing several reasons for her strange illness.

"But we will run the necessary tests, Kayla and determine the cause."

It was not until Kayla and Lydia were almost home that she realized that the physician had told her nothing of sustenance.

I can only wait for the results – however long that will take. In the meanwhile, Daed is working alone on the farm.

Suddenly, another figure appeared, close to the entrance of the maize and Kayla started.

"Hello!" she called out, her brow furrowing with concern. The stranger turned to look at her and he seemed to freeze as they stared at one another.

"Hello," he replied, turning to face her. Kayla stepped back in surprise as he emerged from the stalks, dressed in pair of blue jeans and a black and red flannel shirt.

"Who are you?" she demanded as she stared at him uncomprehendingly. "Does my father know you are here?"

The dark-haired man paused, cocking his head to the side slightly, a single strand of hair falling directly onto his forehead.

"Yes," he answered. "My name is Will. Will Jenkins."

Kayla waited for him to elaborate on why he stood on their land but he did not speak. Slowly, she drew closer to him.

"Why are you on our land?" Kayla asked, her green eyes narrowing in suspicion. She loathed that she was immediately concerned about the Englisher's presence but she could not reconcile one good reason that the man would be on the property.

"I am helping with the harvest," Will told her simply.

"Helping whom?"

Will stared at her for a long moment as if he was concerned she was slow-witted.

"I am helping the owner of the land obviously," he replied dryly. "Who are you?"

Kayla was reluctant to disclose any information to the man, her eyes lifting to see where her father was in the field.

Daed wouldn't hire an Englisher to help on the farm, she thought, distrustful of Will Jenkins. *And he certainly did not mention bringing on any help.*

To her relief, she was Jeremiah approaching.

"There is my father now," Kayla said sternly. "If you do not belong here, you best run along before he catches you on our property."

Will gave her a bemused smile.

"If I ran along, I would not be doing my job," he told her lightly. "I think your father would be angrier at that."

"Kayla you are home," Jeremiah cried, hurrying toward his daughter. She watched as he glanced nervously at the stranger.

"Come inside and we will talk," the senior Roth said, without acknowledging the Englisher in their midst. Kayla opened her mouth to speak but the look in her father's eye silenced her.

"Yes, *Daed*," she agreed, turning to follow Jeremiah inside the house. Will remained in place, his mouth upturned and Kayla cast him one long look before entering the house.

"Daed, did you hire that Englisher to help with the harvest?" she asked dubiously.

"Yes, but that is unimportant. Tell me what the doctor said," Jeremiah told her, abruptly changing the conversation.

"But *Daed*, I will be fine soon. You did not need to hire anyone, especially not an outsider!" Kayla cried.

Jeremiah's mouth became a fine line and his eyes narrowed.

"I do not wish to discuss the Englisher," he told her flatly. "I asked you about the doctor. What was said and what tests were done?"

Kayla swallowed another question.

"She believes that it is a blood disorder of sorts but I will not know until the tests come back. Simple bloodwork was performed. I will return next week for the results."

Jeremiah's brow knitted and he nodded.

"What sort of blood disorder?"

Kayla shrugged.

"I do not know, Daed. She did not give me specifics. I can only wait to learn."

Jeremiah did not seem happy with her answer but Kayla had little else to give him.

"Go rest now, Kayla. I will come to you after the work is done."

"*Daed*, may I go for Hannah? I do not wish to spend one more minute in bed. Please?"

Jeremiah regarded her for a long moment before bobbing his head reluctantly.

"If you are certain you are not feeling ill, you may pick up your sister from school. But you must come straight back to bed. Understood?"

Gratefully, Kayla nodded and hurried toward the front door before he could change his mind.

It will be lovely to stretch my legs and inhale the fresh autumn air, she thought. She was beginning to feel as a caged rabbit.

As she walked toward the road, she found herself looking back at Will Jenkins. He was hard at work, paying her no mind but as she turned in the direction of the schoolhouse, Kayla thought she could feel eyes on her.

Who is this man and what is he doing here?

That evening, Lydia Fisher came as promised, preparing a delicious supper for the Roths before heading home to her own family.

"She is a blessing to us," Jeremiah commented when she left and they sat down to eat. Kayla scowled slightly.

"She really doesn't need be here quite so often, *Daed*," she told her father. "I can still work."

"Your health is paramount, Kayla. Lydia has four able sons to work their farm and can spare a hand until you are well."

"I am well!" Kayla grunted, trying to keep the frustration from her voice. Jeremiah shot her a warning look and Kayla clamped her mouth closed. Arguing would not prove fruitful.

"Tell me about the Englisher," Kayla said instead and Hannah's head jerked upward from her stew.

"What Englisher?" the little girl asked curiously. Jeremiah's scowl deepened and he shook his head almost imperceivably at his oldest daughter.

"I have already explained that Will is helping with the harvest. There is nothing else to tell."

"Where did you find him, *Daed*? You must admit that it is odd to bring an outsider here when there are many in the community whom you could call upon for help."

Jeremiah's blue eyes seemed to darken.

"I am the head of this house," he snapped. "I do not need to answer to you for my choices."

Kayla was stung by his tone and she bit her lower lip. It was unlike her father to speak crossly to her or Hannah.

Whatever silliness is happening with me is causing him stress, she determined, taking a spoonful of beef stew. *I must not give him more of a reason to worry.*

She did not mention Will again but she decided that she would speak to Will the next time she saw him and learn more about him.

Kayla had her chance the following day. Jeremiah went to sell their goods at market, leaving Kayla alone.

"I have asked Lydia to come later in the day to ensure you are well," her father told her. Kayla rolled her eyes where he could not see.

You must not get annoyed, she warned herself but she could not help but feel frustrated at being treated like a child. She knew that was not Jeremiah's intention but she could not release the slight resentment she was feeling.

Her mother had died when she was fourteen, leaving Kayla as the woman of the household. Hannah was still an infant and Kayla had learned to tend to both the baby and the farm.

Standing idle was not something which she did well and she wished desperately that the doctors would quickly diagnose her issue so she was able to resume her role in the family and on the farm.

"Thank you, *Daed,*" she said instead of unleashing the barrage of protests vying to spring from her lips.

"I do not want you to leave the house today, Kayla," Jeremiah told her seriously as he stood in the doorway of her bedroom. "Stay inside and preferably in bed. If you are to faint with no one nearby..."

"I will not faint!" she cried but Jeremiah shook his head.

"You have no way of assuring me of that," he replied. "Please heed my words, Kayla. I speak only out of concern for you."

Begrudgingly, Kayla nodded.

"Yes, *Daed,*" she agreed. "I will take Hannah to school and – "

"No," Jeremiah said sharply. "Lydia will take your sister to school."

Kayla gritted her teeth and nodded.

"Have a good day in town, *Daed,*" Kayla sighed. She watched as he retreated to the freshly loaded wagon and disappeared down the road.

I have become a prisoner in my own home, Kayla thought mournfully, folding her arms across her chest. She wondered what she would do for the remainder of the day and as she thought it, she watched a silver sedan car driving up the road which Jeremiah had just taken.

Kayla leaned forward, watching the dilapidated vehicle pull onto their land, her pulse quickening. As she peered at the driver, she realized it was Will Jenkins arriving to work.

Is he supposed to be here today? She wondered nervously. If so, why hadn't her father told her to expect him.

Will jumped from the driver's seat and she noted he was wearing the same clothes he had the day before. He did not seem to notice her observing him, pulling a few items which she could not see from the backseat before turning toward the barn.

As Kayla rose her hand to wave in greeting, something tugged on her skirt.

"Kayla, I am hungry!" Hannah announced from behind her, causing the older girl to jump.

"You startled me, Hannah!" she chided and Hannah shrugged indifferently. She turned to usher her sister into the house, eyeing Will who had vanished behind the house.

I wonder if I should tend to him, she thought but her father's words reverberated in her mind.

"I do not want you to leave the house today, Kayla. Stay inside and preferably in bed. If you are to faint with no one nearby..."

She pushed the thought of Will Jenkins from her mind and closed the door.

She had no reason to approach the Englisher.

The weather had turned unseasonably warm and Kayla lifted her head from her book, realizing that the front room had grown almost stifling hot.

She cast the novel aside and reached to open the window, gazing into the fields. To her surprise, she saw Will Jenkins standing near the maple tree beside his car, wiping sweat from his brow.

Kayla watched him for a moment and she could see the sun and hard work had turned his face red.

He must be thirsty. He is dressed much too warmly to work the fields in that attire, she realized, rising from window seat.

A cool glass of water in hand, Kayla stepped into the yard. Will's back was to her and she tried to make herself heard as to not surprise him.

He turned and Kayla was filled with a strange sense of familiarity suddenly, something she had not felt the previous afternoon.

"Hello," he said and Kayla nodded, handing him the glass of water.

"It is very hot today," she volunteered. "I thought you might be thirsty."

He nodded gratefully and accepted the beverage, drinking it in one long gulp.

"I will fetch you another one," she offered and he shook his head.

"No, thank you," he replied. "I should be getting back to work."

He was older than Kayla with dark hair and vivid green eyes. His face seemed it had not been shaved in four days and there were dark circles under his eyes.

He is handsome in a rugged sort of way, she thought, studying his face. The feeling that she knew him did not diminish.

"As you wish," she replied, turning back.

"Actually wait," Will called nervously. He peered at his gloved hands in embarrassment as Kayla turned back to him.

"Yes?"

"Maybe one more glass of water," he muttered and Kayla smiled.

"Of course."

Inside the house, she thought of the somewhat bedraggled man on her lawn and she again wondered where he had come from.

If he has no water, he likely has no food either, she realized and quickly went to work preparing him a snack. *If he doesn't eat, he will also faint. Daed doesn't need to come home to such a sight.*

She did not want to think what her father would say if he knew she was feeding the Englisher.

Outside, she gestured for him to sit and eat. The gratitude in his face was beyond anything she had ever seen and a mixture of sadness and pity overwhelmed her.

"Are you from Lancaster, Mr. Jenkins?" Kayla asked timidly as he inhaled the bread and cheese she had brought to him. He shook his head and she waited for him to swallow the morsels before answering.

"No," he replied. "I am from Reading."

Kayla's brow furrowed.

"Reading?" she asked in surprise. "You have a little bit of a journey to make here."

Will nodded and shrugged his shoulders.

"It is an hour's drive," he answered. "But your father offered me very good pay and gas money for the trip."

None of what he said made sense to Kayla.

Why would Daed bring an Englisher to the district from an hour away?

"You know, I don't even know your name," Will commented as he polished off the last of the light meal she provided for him.

Embarrassed, Kayla extended her hand.

"Kayla Roth."

Will accepted her outstretched palm and they two looked at one another for a long moment. Kayla felt a sudden confusion as she stared at him.

Why do I feel such an affinity with this man? She wondered, an almost awe-struck feeling overcoming her.

"Nice to meet you, Kayla. I should be getting back to work. I don't want your dad to think he's wasting his money."

Kayla stepped back reluctantly, wanting to speak with him longer but she knew he was right. There was much work to be done and she had detained the harvest enough already.

"If you should need more water, Mr. Jenkins," Kayla told him. "There is a spigot beside the barn."

He looked at her thankfully.

"You truly are a lifesaver, Miss Roth. You and your father have helped me a great deal already."

Kayla did not know how to respond but Will did not seem to require an answer.

She slipped back into the house and reclaimed her window seat but her book was forgotten. She spent the remainder of the afternoon watching Will working in the field and wondering if *Gotte* had sent him to their farm for a reason.

Kayla waited impatiently for her father to take Hannah to school before hurrying outside to greet Will who was cleaning the stalls. Her father would not be gone long but she wanted to talk to the man again, if only for a short time.

"Good morning, Miss Roth," Will said brightly. She smiled.

"You may call me Kayla," she told him. "I brought you muffins if you are hungry."

She offered them to him and he took them happily. For the third day, he donned the same clothes and Kayla wondered if he had any other garments.

He is obviously not well off. I wonder if that is why Daed brought him here; to help a man down on his luck.

"In that case, you can call me Will," he laughed, taking a bite of the muffin in his hand. His dark eyebrows shot up.

"This is great!" he said. "Did you make this yourself?"

She nodded.

"The Amish can do everything," he sighed. "I knew an Amish girl once. She never failed to amaze me with her talents."

"What happened to her?" Kayla asked curiously, leaning against a stall door. Will smiled thinly.

"She returned to her community. Decided the outside world wasn't for her after all."

Kayla could read the regret in his face but before she could ask anything else, she felt herself grow lightheaded.

Oh no! She thought as bright lights colored her line of sight.

"Kayla?" Will's voice sounded very far away and suddenly she was in his arms as her legs buckled beneath her. She willed herself to take deep breaths and to her relief she did not faint.

"Are you all right?" Will demanded as she regained her footing. Slowly he released her and Kayla stood on shaking legs.

She nodded, shifting her eyes downward.

"I get fainting spells sometimes," she confessed as the spots cleared from her vision. Will's emerald eyes narrowed.

"Have you been to the doctor?" he asked and Kayla bobbed her head.

"I am awaiting test results," she told him, sighing. "They believe it is some sort of blood disorder."

Will's mouth became a tight, white line.

"Is that so?" he asked quietly.

"Kayla! What are you doing in here?" Jeremiah appeared in the doorway, his face pale as he took in the scene before him.

"I – I came to offer Mr. Jenkins some muffins," she murmured, averting her eyes from his shocked face.

"You should not be in here," he told his daughter, shooing her from the barn.

"Thank you for the muffins, Kayla," Will called after her. "I hope you are feeling better."

Jeremiah led the way back to the house and did not say a word until they were inside, whirling to confront Kayla.

"Why were you speaking with Will Jenkins?" he demanded furiously. "I told you that you are to stay in the house."

"Daed, I am growing mad staying in the house!" Kayla protested. "And Will seems a very nice man!"

Jeremiah's expression was indecipherable as he stared at his oldest daughter. He seemed to be considering his next words carefully.

"You are to stay away from Will Jenkins," he told her firmly. "I do not want you anywhere near him, do you understand?"

Kayla's eyebrows knit together.

"No," she answered truthfully. "Of course I do not understand. Why would you ask me to stay away from him?"

"He is not someone whom you should associate yourself," Jeremiah insisted. Kayla stared at him uncomprehendingly.

"*Daed*, if he is such a terrible man, why would you have him come to our home?"

"He not in our home. He is merely helping with harvest. I want you to swear that you will not have any further contact with him. Swear it, Kayla!"

Kayla did not know what to say. She wanted to promise her father that she wouldn't see the Englisher again but she knew her curiosity would not keep her away.

"Kayla!"

She hung her head and nodded, sighing deeply.

"I swear it, *Daed*," she breathed but she wondered if she would be able to honor her oath.

Kayla did not risk going to Will until the next time her father went to the market, three days later. She found herself watching the worker from the window often, willing him to take notice of her and sometimes he would lift his head and acknowledge her with a half-wave but never in Jeremiah's presence.

This makes little sense. Daed brings him from out of town to work and then speaks as if the man is a danger to us.

The previous day, she had gone to the hospital for her test results.

"As we suspected, Kayla, you have a blood disorder called megaloblastic anemia. It can be treated with supplements and dietary changes but it is manageable," the doctor informed her. Kayla nodded, relieved the diagnosis was simple.

"When will I be able to resume my work?" she asked eagerly and the doctor chuckled.

"We will start your injections immediately and you should notice a change within a week or so. The fatigue and dizziness will lessen and you will be back to normal in no time."

Kayla peered at the physician.

"What causes this?" she asked with interest.

"In your case, it is genetic," the doctor replied.

After Hannah left for school and her father for the market, Kayla rushed outside to speak with Will.

"Kayla, you should not be out here," he told her, his jaw locking when she appeared. Kayla was hurt by his words.

"I do not understand; why does my father wish to keep me away from you?" she asked bluntly but Will did not answer as he continued to bale hay.

"I'm sorry," she muttered, turning away. "I only came to tell you that I got my results from the hospital. I have a blood disorder – anemia."

Will's head jerked up to stare at her, his mouth open slightly.

"What kind of anemia?" he demanded. Kayla wracked her mind to recall the proper term.

"Mega...mega..."

"Megaloblastic?"

Kayla smiled.

"Yes, that is it."

Kayla waited for him to return her grin but his face went dark.

"You should go back in the house. You don't want your father to catch you out here."

She stared at him, tears of humiliation filling her eyes.

I thought we had a bond, she thought miserably, chewing on her lower lip.

"Hurry up," Will growled, pointing at the house. Kayla spun, tears spilling down her cheeks as she ran back inside.

Daed was right; I should have just stayed away from him.

"Kayla! *Daed* is yelling!" Hannah cried, flying into the kitchen where Kayla was doing the dishes.

"What?"

"He is yelling at the Englisher!" Hannah insisted, pointing toward the front of the house. Kayla quickly dried her hands on her apron and rushed toward the door. As she pulled open the heavy wood, she heard a car door slam and watched as Will screeched away in his rundown sedan.

Jeremiah stood, his arms folded angrily across his chest as he watched the man leave and Kayla was sure she had never seen him look so intimidating.

"*Daed*! *Daed,* what happened?" she cried, rushing toward him. He whirled to face her, his face undergoing several expressions, settling on near-panic.

"Nothing," he replied gruffly. "Go inside."

"*Daed* please!" she begged. "What happened with Will?"

His eyes narrowed dangerously and he shook his head.

"I made a mistake bringing him here," he muttered, storming toward the house. "Do not mention his name in this house again."

Bewildered, Kayla turned toward the road but of course Will was long gone.

She looked helplessly at her father but she was only staring at his retreating back and Kayla was filled with an inexplicable sense of loss.

He is not coming back, she realized and the thought made her sick to her stomach for reasons she could not comprehend.

Life on the Roth farm returned to normal and as promised, Kayla began to feel better as the treatments took effect.

The harvest went well and Will Jenkins did not return to the district but his memory was fresh in Kayla's mind.

Perhaps one day, Daed will tell me who he was truly and how he came to be here. But she did not have high hopes for that occurring. Jeremiah never brought up the Englisher again and Kayla did not dare.

It was the beginning of November when the letter arrived.

It was slipped between the screen door and it had not been mailed.

Without opening it, Kayla suspected she knew who had written it but as she tore into the envelope, her suspicions were confirmed.

Her hands trembling, she read the letter, her heart thumping wildly.

Dear Kayla, it read. *I have wrestled with whether to write this letter or leave well enough alone as your father wanted. I can't live my life without telling you who I am because I think you deserve the truth. As you know, my name is William Jenkins. Twenty years ago, I met a beautiful girl in Lancaster and we fell madly in love. I mentioned that I once knew an Amish girl and that girl was your mother, Anna. We had plans to marry but one day, I woke up and she was gone. She had left me a letter, much like the one I am writing you, apologizing for her choice and claiming she had made a mistake leaving her community. She begged me not to look for her and I agreed. I left town and moved to Reading, not wanting to run into her. If I had stayed, I would have learned that she married Jeremiah Roth and soon gave birth to a beautiful baby daughter; you.*

If I had not seen your eyes, I may never have known that you were mine but there is no mistaking you are my child.

I did not understand why your father had brought me to your farm until I heard you were sick. Megaloblastic anemia is genetic – I know because I have it also. I suspect Jeremiah was terribly concerned for your health and wanted to learn about your family history. I don't think he ever intended for us to meet and when we did and I learned the truth, he grew angry and banished me from the farm. I want you to know that if I had known you were my child, I would have always been in your life.

You may do what you wish with this information, Kayla. You may choose to never see me again or you may confront your father. Shamefully I do not know you well enough to know how you will react but I would like to get to know you. You are a grown woman and I can't force a relationship on you.

Whatever you do, please remember that your father only did what he did to keep you safe, happy and healthy. If you decide to let him know that you know, go easy on him. He is the only father you have ever had after all.

I have enclosed my phone number and mailing address. I will not hold my breath but I will hold onto hope that you will see me again.

Whatever you choose, know that I support you and love you. I wish you only the best this world has to offer.

Love always,

Will

Tears flowed freely down Kayla's face and the words grew blurry as she read and re-read the letter, her breath escaping in shuddering sobs.

"Oh Gotte, Kayla!" Jeremiah cried, entering the foyer where his oldest daughter stood. "What happened?"

Kayla shook her head and stuffed the letter back into the envelope, wiping her face with the back of her hand.

"Nothing, nothing," she gasped. He stared at her, his face a mask of worry and Kayla had never been filled with so much love for another person.

Does he know I know? Has he been filled with worry for the past nineteen years that the truth would come out and he would lose the daughter he had raised as his own? Kayla could not imagine the pain her father must have endured over the years.

He is the only father I have ever known. He is my Daed no matter what that letter reads.

Impulsively, she threw herself into her father's arm, burying her face in his broad chest.

"I love you, *Daed*," she whispered, inhaling the comforting scent of his dirty work clothes.

"I love you, daughter," he sighed.

In that moment, Kayla knew she would honor her father's wishes and never again bring up Will Jenkin's name in their home.

That did not mean she would never see the Englischer again.

AN AMISH FRIENDSHIP

85

ERICA FANNING

Living in the Plain community was an absolute joy. In the spring and summer, there were parties and get-togethers in the town square. Young love was in the air and many weddings were conducted. In the fall was the harvest time, where the community would come together as always and help everyone to make sure nothing was left unharvested. Much of what was made and harvested was sold on market days to Englishers passing through from one big city to another. What wasn't sold was saved and stored for the community and for each respective family to help them through the harsh winter. Being in the northeastern part of the country made each winter unpredictable, but they always made their way through it and began to prepare for as many contingencies as possible.

No one could prepare for the contingency of what was about to come upon them.

Rebecca Miller did her usual winter morning duties before the rest of the family was up: feeding the chickens, gathering their eggs, and making sure they were warm. She also checked the garden one last time. It hadn't snowed yet this year, but the ominous clouds above her head and the cold north wind threatened it at any moment. She pulled the shawl she was wearing a little tighter and noticed that there were a few extra vegetables her little brother had missed in his excitement over the stray dog in their yard yesterday. She smiled remembering his little face light up as he ran toward the strange creature. Rebecca's father, Joseph Miller, wouldn't allow the family to get a dog unless they could find one with the right temperament to guard the chickens. Little Matthew was bound and determined that the dog he found was the one.

"I don't think that's how it works, buddy," Rebecca had said. "Besides, this one has a rope around his neck. He probably belongs to someone." Rebecca wasn't going to mention to Matthew that the bullmastiff's massive head gave her some unease. *That thing could eat you alive,* is what she had wanted to say, but instead she went with, "Let's get you inside. If he's still here when we're done with snack, then we'll talk to Papa about keeping him."

Matthew had been disappointed, but he agreed.

Today, the silence in the air made it seem like not another soul on the earth even existed. Any moment now, it was going to snow. Rebecca hurried inside and no sooner had she walked inside and the snow slowly began falling.

Rebecca loved the snow, it always gave the earth a sort of "do-over" look. She watched it for a few moments before realizing her arms were full of vegetables and eggs. She watched the snow a few seconds more, and then went about her chores for the day.

By mid-afternoon, the snow had been falling steadily now. Matthew was more than excited and wanted to go play with his friends. Papa wouldn't allow it because the Miller's didn't have proper winter attire.

"I don't need you getting sick, my son."

Only three winters ago, Mary Miller, their beloved wife and mother, passed away from pneumonia. Rebecca wasn't above taking her into the nearest town to get medical help, but Papa strictly forbade it.

"No," he had said. "The Miller's haven't been to an English community in over a hundred and fifty years. We're not about to start now. God will heal your Mama."

Both Rebecca and Matthew—who had only been 8 at the time—were scarred toward God and anything taught in church for a long time. Since Matthew was younger, he was able to accept that maybe God allowed it to happen because of some hidden sin that he didn't know about. Rebecca knew better. A loving God wouldn't allow any of His children to be harmed like that. He wouldn't allow a woman who loved Him almost as much as King David in the Bible to be brought down with one of the worst illnesses known to the Plain community. No, she decided she would stay within the community for her little brother, but she wouldn't really serve this supposed God that caused her mother to die.

In fact, most of the time, snow caused her to think very fondly of her mother and how much she loved snow. When it snowed, it was hard for Rebecca to think anything ill toward anyone. She smiled at Matthew trying to convince her to help change Papa's mind.

"Silly boy," she laughed. "You're not going to be able to convince him to let you out. Maybe in the springtime, we'll start making winter clothing so you can go play with your friends next year."

"But that's next year," Matthew pouted. "Maybe James' family has something extra. Please, Rebecca? Can't we at least go ask?"

Rebecca sighed and looked at her father who was standing in the doorway of the living room, where his two children were. He nodded once. She smiled at her little brother. "Let's go."

As soon as Rebecca set a booted foot outside the front door, she knew this snow wasn't going to let up anytime soon. In fact, in the short amount of time it took her and Matthew to get to their neighbors, there was already another quarter of an inch of snow on the ground. As soon as Naphtali Fisher saw the young Miller's out in the snow, she ran outside and covered them both in an extra shawl.

"What do you two think you're doing?" She scolded them as soon as they were inside. "This snow is accumulating so quickly, and Matthew is so little he could get stuck!"

"Mrs. Fisher, I want to play outside with James," Matthew announced as if Naphtali hadn't said anything. "Do you have any extra winter clothes for me?" He looked at her waiting, as she looked at Rebecca in disbelief.

"You came all the way here so he could ask to play out in this?" She looked at Matthew. "No, dear. James is sick. He has the flu. I don't want you to get sick either; maybe you should stay here with us."

"Oh no," Rebecca interjected before Matthew could say anything. "If there's someone sick here, it might be better if we head back. Besides, Papa would be worried for us. Thank you."

Naphtali insisted they take the extra shawls and simply return them when they could. Naphtali was a seamstress by trade and by hobby. Their house was never short of clothing or anything made of fabric.

"You mustn't go by yourselves," Mrs. Fisher insisted one last time. "Luke!" She called for her oldest son and he came around the corner in a flash.

"Yes, Mama?" It had been months since Rebecca had seen Luke Fisher, but she didn't remember him being that handsome. He was well-toned in his body, and he had a lean face with gentle brown eyes underneath a full head of wavy brown hair.

It took Rebecca a moment to realize she had stopped breathing. She knew Mrs. Fisher and Matthew were both talking to her, but she simply remembered walking out the door and it wasn't until they were halfway home that she realized Luke was right there next to her, guiding her steps and making small talk. She knew she was responding, but couldn't remember any of the conversation they had. She did remember him wishing her a goodnight and telling her he would see her in the morning at church.

Church? She didn't realize tomorrow was a church day. "Papa, there's church tomorrow?"

Papa laughed. "I would hope so, my dear. It's Sunday. I know it's not too late, but would you go check on the chickens one last time before it gets too dark?"

Rebecca obeyed, and while she was out there, she tried desperately to remember what she and Luke had talked about on the way home, but all she was coming up with was the way his voice sounded and how steady his hands were whenever she lost her balance. It wasn't until today that she realized having a mate in her life would be an amazing experience, and she hoped that it would be Luke. She was only 16, but she knew she was ready for marriage because that's what the Plain community taught its young women to be prepared for. Rebecca had mastered much of what her mother had taught her in the three years since she had left this earth.

She decided staying outside with the chickens much longer was a bad idea because the wind began to pick up and kick a lot of the snow about. She locked the pen up tightly so the door wouldn't fly open with the wind and quickly returned inside.

"Papa, the weather's starting to get really bad outside. Do you think they'll even had church tomorrow?" Rebecca didn't want to try to travel in this weather if she could avoid it.

"Well, if they ring the bell, then we'll know." The bell was used to assemble the churchgoers, but in extreme cases like this, it was used as a warning to stay where they were. But no sooner had he finished speaking and the church bell rung.

"Quickly! Get as much as you can: food, blankets, clothing. We're going to the church."

The snow was so deep, Matthew kept getting stuck. Papa finally had to carry him to the church. When they arrived, it was already almost full to the brim of people who lived closer than the Miller's.

"How are they going to fit everyone in here?" Rebecca asked absently. Just then Luke Fisher came up to them.

"The basement is open for those who are sick. We still plan on having church in the morning, but we might just move the pews tonight to make room for makeshift beds. Mr. Miller, the men are meeting on the stage to talk about a plan. Would you be willing to help us?"

Papa looked at Rebecca and she nodded. She would stay with Matthew while he helped the men.

"Come, Matthew. Let's get out of the doorway." Rebecca moved them to a warm spot in the sanctuary. There were already a lot of people there, but Rebecca knew they were going to have to get cozy if they wanted to stay alive.

"Excuse me everyone!" It was Luke. Rebecca wasn't sure where the preacher was, but people seemed to listen to Luke just as well. It became quiet except for the people that were still coming in. "Thank you all for coming. Preacher Hostetler has informed me that they are predicting this weather to be some of the worst we've seen in over a hundred years." There were murmurs in the crowd. People were getting nervous.

"There's no need to worry. We have a food stash in the cellar and it looks like some of the other women of the community have brought their own food. We won't ask you to share, but if you want to do so, anything you can give to the community would be greatly appreciated.

"Now, we're still figuring out the logistics of how we're going to bed everyone in here. We want to keep the basement for those who are sick, but we will need volunteers to help care for them. If that's something you want to do, please come stand to the left of the stage."

Rebecca knew in her heart that's what she wanted to do, but she couldn't leave Matthew all alone. She looked at her father, who was standing within visual range, and she caught his eye. He glanced at the growing throng of women, then looked at her and cocked his head. He was okay with her going as long as Matthew stayed put.

"Matthew, I need you to stay here with Miss Mary." The young schoolteacher had been sitting there and had seen the exchange between Rebecca and her father.

"Don't worry about him. He'll be fine," she assured her. Rebecca thanked her and hurried over with the group. As soon as she got over there, Luke announced that they had an ample amount of women and would need others to help cook for the healthy.

"With this many people, it's going to take community effort to make sure we all get out of this alive." Luke continued giving directions for a few more minutes and then dismissed everyone to go to their stations.

Mrs. Stoltzfus was the oldest woman in the group of caretakers, so she quickly took charge and began ordering everyone about as soon as they got to the basement. Since it was late in the evening, they were simply trying to make sure that the sick were comfortable and then began making arrangements for food to be brought down as soon as possible. Rebecca was the youngest of the caretakers, so she did a lot of the running up and down the stairs to make sure the communication stayed open between the floors and the leaders. Basically, she became the messenger girl. She didn't mind so much because that gave her an excuse to see Luke more often and even to talk to him.

By midnight, Rebecca was exhausted and just wanted to sleep. Mrs. Stoltzfus noticed her fatigue and sent her upstairs to sleep with her family. She didn't argue and was glad for the short respite.

When Rebecca woke up the next morning, her throat was on fire and she felt dizzy. She thought nothing of it as she took a swig of some water, washed her face, and hurried downstairs to help. It felt cooler than she remembered and her body shivered. As soon as Mrs. Stoltzfus saw her, she made her sit down.

"Child, you don't look well." The older woman felt Rebecca's forehead. "In fact, you have a fever. Here, we have an extra bed for you right next to James Fisher." Mrs. Stoltzfus led her to the bed and helped her lie down. "I might need your help, but I do believe you're coming down with the flu. It would be best if you stayed still and let the fever pass."

"No, Mrs. Stoltzfus," Rebecca tried to argue. "I'm fine. I think it's just because I didn't sleep well last night. I'll be fine." Mrs. Stoltzfus pushed her down.

"No, child," she insisted. "You stay right there." She helped Rebecca take her shoes off and pulled a blanket up to her chin. "If I see you get up, I will tie you down to this bed."

James Fisher snickered at that. "Oooh, Rebecca's in trouble." He laughed again which led to a coughing fit.

"Now, now," Mrs. Stoltzfus turned from Rebecca to focus on James' coughing. "You must be careful child. Here," she handed him some herbal tea that had been by his bed. "Drink this and your throat will feel better."

"But it's cold."

"I'll go make you some new tea while I cook some up for Miss Miller." She scurried off, making sure to tell some of the other caretakers to keep an eye on Rebecca and James as she went to make more tea.

Rebecca sat up as soon as she was out of sight and kicked the blanket off. "I can't stay here."

"Heh, well don't let Mrs. Stoltzfus find out you're getting up," a voice behind her stated. She spun around to see James' oldest brother Luke standing there, arms folded. "She seemed pretty serious about tying you to the bed."

"You heard that?" Rebecca asked quietly. Luke laughed and nodded as her face flushed. James laughed with his brother.

"Actually, she had to tie me down too, and I've been sick for a week." James seemed very excited about this. "But I know I'm getting better. I already feel like I could run a race!"

Luke went over to his brother's bed and sat on it. "That's great, but you know Mrs. Stoltzfus won't let you go until we can get an actual doctor in here to make sure you're alright."

"Wait," Rebecca stopped him. "We're having an actual doctor come in?" Luke sighed sadly.

"There's almost two feet of snow outside. I don't think anyone's coming for a few days... but last night Mrs. Stoltzfus asked me if I would call a doctor in so that we don't lose people to simple illnesses that the English medical community has found cures for." He lowered his voice before adding, "Like your mother."

Rebecca felt her chest tighten. All those questions of why's and what if's suddenly came back and flooded her thoughts. Suddenly she couldn't catch her breath. Luke had laid her down and was standing over her. He was yelling something, but all she could hear was the quickening sound of her heart, struggling to get oxygen to her brain. The edges of Rebecca's vision began to blur just as Mrs. Stoltzfus came up and sat her up. She was telling her to breathe. She began counting: 1, 2, 3, 4,... The feeling passed as quickly as it came.

"Good job," Mrs. Stoltzfus smiled calmly. "Take a few deep breaths slowly. Do you feel alright now?" Rebecca nodded slowly.

"Rebecca, I am so sorry," Luke said apologetically. "I had no intention of hurting you—"

"Stop." Rebecca didn't want to hear it right now. She just wanted to sleep. She began to lie back, but Mrs. Stoltzfus kept her sitting up.

"You have to drink this first." She handed Rebecca the herbal tea with lemon and honey. Rebecca took a few sips and thanked the woman, who looked at Luke and told him sternly it was time to leave.

Luke looked defeated and helpless, but wasn't about to argue. Slowly, he walked toward the stairs and out of sight.

"Whatever he said to you, honey, don't let it affect you." Mrs. Stoltzfus placed her hand gently on Rebecca's arm. "Sometimes people don't understand what it's like to lose someone they love. He didn't mean anything he said in a harsh way." Rebecca nodded.

"I know," she responded quietly. "It wasn't what he said, but the thoughts that came with it. What happened to me?" The lead caretaker smiled warmly.

"Something we're going to avoid from happening ever again."

As the days went on, some of the younger sick ones began to get better, James and Rebecca among those. As soon as Rebecca was better, she began helping as a caretaker again. She needed something to do to keep her mind off of the fact that they were still stuck in the church. It had been five days and the snow still hadn't let up. Some of the snowbanks were well over ten feet tall and the church doors had been snowed in by day two of the storms. Thankfully the entire community had managed to fit well into the little church place, but many of them were beginning to wonder why they hadn't seen the preacher or his family. Rumors had begun flying that they had gotten stuck in the parish next door. They saw lights on every night from what little could be seen out the windows.

Every night the community got together to pray for the preacher, for the county, for the community's animals that had been left unattended and even for the surrounding English communities. Perhaps they had amenities that the Plain community didn't, but as Luke pointed out during prayer one night, they were still struggling with the same elements and they didn't prepare every year like the community did.

Although Rebecca had been upset by what Luke had said, she also saw how hurt he was by what he had said. She made it a point to go out of her way to talk to him one day during lunch.

"May I sit with you?" She asked politely after she found him sitting alone. He looked up and nodded, his mind seemingly somewhere else. "Are you alright?"

"No," he finally admitted. "The preacher... I know where he is, and it's not next door." Rebecca waited for more, but finally had to ask him to elaborate. "The preacher is the one that went to get a doctor to come look at the sick. I haven't heard from him or anyone, and the cellular phone he provided hasn't had service in three days. I don't want to be depressing, but I don't think he's even alive." He looked up at Rebecca and she saw that he had tears in his eyes. "I'm afraid, Rebecca."

She moved around to his side of the table and held him as he began to cry. The sat like that for a long time before someone called Luke's name. He quickly sat up and wiped his face.

"I have to go."

"I understand." Rebecca was upset that she wasn't able to talk to him, but she knew in her heart that she had forgiven him.

"Thank you," he said as he looked into her eyes, fresh tears welling up. "I feel like I can trust you, and I have always appreciated that about you, Rebecca Miller." He got up and left her sitting there alone.

She knew in her heart that she would never forget this moment... and she would never tell anyone where the preacher really was. She sent up a quick prayer for his safety and hoped he'd made it to town before the storm had gotten too bad, but like Luke she felt in her heart that it was probably too late for him. And that would be the most painful thing for the community to accept.

The next morning, the snow had finally stopped and the sun was shining. It helped to heat the little church some, since there was still so much snow on the windows. The community was abuzz with excitement about how soon they might be able to leave and get back to their abodes to assess the damage. Luke assured everyone that as soon as they could dig their way out of the church and onto the road, people could begin leaving. They were going to have to stay in the church a few more days before that happened though. The men were still putting a plan together on what the next steps were to be.

Indeed, it was another five cold days in the church before the men began to dig a way out of the church. The congregation cheered, and since Rebecca was downstairs helping with the sick, she was sent to see what was happening. The news brought so much hope into the room that many of the sick seemed to get better just by hearing it.

"We need to begin making preparations to leave as soon as possible," Mrs. Stoltzfus told Rebecca and another young girl. "Begin packing everything that we don't absolutely need—any extra bandages, extra tea, that sort of thing. Quickly now!"

"Make way!"

Suddenly there was a hustling coming down the stairs and the three women were almost forced out of the way. There were two men—Luke and Mr. Miller—carrying someone between them... the preacher!

Without any more pleading, Rebecca and the other girl went and retrieved as many extra blankets as they could. The preacher—Troyer—was blue, but he was still breathing. He was wrapped in blankets of his own and had a hat and mittens on, but they didn't know how long he'd been outside.

A crowd had begun forming around the small bed and on the stairs as people were clamoring to see their beloved preacher. Mrs. Stoltzfus shooed them all away with a word and went back to peeling the frozen clothes off of the preacher.

"Set up a curtain for us," she told Rebecca. "We don't need prying eyes to see what our beloved preacher is going through." She ran off to find Naphtali Fisher, the seamstress. She had brought a whole bag of extra blankets and shawls. Maybe she had something to use as curtains.

She found the woman upstairs helping Miss Mary corral the children away from the door in an attempt to keep them warm. There were still men digging their way to the road... Rebecca wasn't sure why the door was still open. She asked them as soon as she reached them.

Naphtali hissed, "I'm not sure, but whoever left it open is about to receive the wrath of God." Rebecca almost forgot why she was there, but as soon as she remembered she spoke in quick sentences. Immediately Naphtali's countenance changed and she went to work finding as much material as she could to help Rebecca make the curtains she needed.

"God bless you child, and God help our preacher." She seemed on the verge of tears; apparently she had been one of the few who hadn't been informed of the new developments. Rebecca nodded and ran down the stairs and began setting up the curtains for more privacy. Mrs. Stoltzfus had the preacher almost completely undressed, and it didn't look good.

She wanted to know how long he had been out there, and where exactly "there" was. Why was he outside by himself? Why didn't he call for help? The questions began forming faster than she could stop them. Her chest began to tighten again and her vision became blurry.

Mrs. Stoltzfus caught it in time and said calmly but firmly, "Breathe, child." Rebecca began counting: *1, 2, 3, 4,...* She took a few deep breaths and hurriedly finished her task.

As soon as she finished, she ran back upstairs to find out why the door was still open. She couldn't find anyone to ask, but the sun on her skin felt nice and warm despite the chill of the winter air. She basked in it only a moment before closing the door firmly and making sure it would still be accessible and easy to open. Luke appeared as soon as she walked away from the door.

"Why did you close the door?" He seemed upset; under the circumstances, that was understandable.

"Because it's cold outside and we don't want the entire community to get sick."

"But we need it open so we can go in and out easily."

"If you need to keep a door open because of convenience, then you shouldn't be living here. There's an English town less than an hour away that will take your convenience. But here, you have to work a little harder to get what you want." Luke pulled back. Rebecca was shocked that even came out of her mouth. "I'm so sorry, I—"

"No," Luke pushed past her, nostrils flaring. "You're not." He slammed the door on his way out, causing those closest to the front of the church to focus their attention on Rebecca. She looked down and walked away as if nothing had happened, but inside she felt as if her world was falling apart. She had no idea how she could possibly have any feelings for Luke Fisher despite all of the things that had happened these past twelve days. She tried to push all of the thoughts out of her mind as she went back downstairs to help Mrs. Stoltzfus and the preacher.

Within a day, a snowplow from the English town had come through and cleared a lot of the snow off of the main road, making the possibility of going home closer than ever. Some people were anxious to what their homes would look like, others were concerned about the animals they'd hastily left behind, but there wasn't one soul who didn't first fear for the future of their preacher and what his fate would be.

A doctor from the English town also came the same day as the snowplow. Luke had managed to get signal on his cellular phone to call the hospital. When the doctor arrived, he immediately called for an ambulance.

"This man has extreme hypothermia. It is literally a miracle that he's still alive. How did this happen?"

Mr. Miller answered, "We found him stuck in a snowbank less than twenty feet outside the door. We don't even know how long he was there. Is he going to make it?"

The doctor shook his head. "I don't know. The damage seems too extensive. I'm not going to make any promises just yet."

Within a few days, they knew the answer. The preacher had passed on. The hypothermia had affected his internal organs too much and nothing they did would fix it.

Luke Fisher was most affected by this, next to the preacher's family. Luke had been mentored by the preacher and was hoping to one day be a preacher in a town of his own one day. Rebecca did what she could to console Luke, but ever since their episode at the church door, Luke had been distant.

With the passing of the preacher and the assessing of their community, everyone's spirits were down. Nearly all the farm animals survived, but the bullmastiff that Matthew had found wandering had died in a snowbank, forever lost to his owners. Matthew cried when Rebecca informed him.

"Why didn't the owners take him back?" There was little consoling the heart of an 11-year-old. Rebecca knew he would bounce back quickly.

There was a lot of damage to houses and to the schoolhouse. Even the church had sustained some damage. Luke took charge and rallied everyone together for one last supper before they officially returned to their homes to rebuild.

Rebecca felt that this would be the best time to try to talk to him before they were simply neighbors again. The way he had treated her for the past week had hurt her every single time she saw him.

"Luke," she began after she came up to the table he was seated at with the preacher's family. She nodded to them and apologized for their loss. "Can we talk in private?"

He didn't seem eager to talk, but he didn't say no. They found a quiet corner and she just let all of her feelings out.

"From the time you walked me home on the first day of snow, to the last argument we had... and everything in between, I've realized something." She stopped and looked away from his face, afraid that she wouldn't be able to finish if she had to look in his eyes for another second.

She continued, "You've been strong, courageous, bold, caring, and passionate. I... I was wondering how you would feel about us courting." She waited a moment before raising her eyes to meet his. She was shocked to see tears streaming down his face, which was soft and tender in that moment.

"Oh Rebecca," he spoke her name as if it was the greatest name in the world. "From the moment your brother became friends with mine, I knew this moment would come. I so desperately wanted you to love me, but was too afraid to do anything because you were going through such a hard time with..." he trailed off, probably afraid Rebecca would have one of her panic attacks. She nodded in understanding.

"Go on."

He moved closer to her, closing the already small gap between them. Her breathing became shallow, but not in the way it had in the past. This was a new feeling. What was this?

"Rebecca Miller," Luke stated, his face only inches from her. "I would love to court you." He kissed her lightly on the lips and a thousand butterflies went off in her stomach at that moment. As quickly as he kissed her, it was over, leaving Rebecca wanting so much more. Luke smiled, seeing the disappointment and confusion on her face.

"You're still only sixteen." He winked. "We'll work up to something better."

"You..." she didn't even know what to say, so she punched him playfully on the arm. He laughed.

"Come on, you should meet the Troyer's."

It was a wonderful thing to see the community come together in their time of mourning and rebuilding. They decided to work on the church and the parish first, since those were the most important buildings in the community. Then they moved onto different barns where the most food was stored. Luke had decided the plan of action would then include working on the houses of the older members of the community, and then those with the youngest children. If the community worked on one thing at the same time, it was accomplished a lot faster. Within two weeks, it was as if nothing had even ravaged the community.

Almost, anyway.

The community was still out a preacher, but the bishop had allowed Luke to preach until they could find a suitable preacher, the Troyer's had to find somewhere else to live, and the community was still mourning the death of their lost shepherd.

Joseph Miller allowed the Troyer's to live with them until a house could be built, so the house suddenly became very full. With Matthew and Rebecca, plus the three young Troyer children, there were five children under the age of 18. Ms. Troyer helped Rebecca with a lot of the cleaning and cooking duties, while Matthew would entertain the children. Mr. Miller was out fixing his barn and tending to his regular winter duties most of the day, so it gave the women some time to talk.

Rebecca could tell that Ms. Troyer was starting to become fond of her father and sometimes she even dropped hints to her Papa that such a thing was happening.

"Papa, you can't shrug this off forever. Mama would want you to be happy and live your life."

"But Rebecca, I am happy. I have my two wonderful children. What else could I need?" Rebecca knew that now was the time to tell him about her and Luke.

"Papa, I won't be here forever." He looked at her, concerned.

"Why?" She laughed.

"Well I'm not dying. Papa, Luke and I are courting! We could be married within the next year! With your permission, of course."

He looked at her for a moment before staring into his hands as if the answer would materialize.

"I don't know what to say," he spoke with a gruff voice. "But I know that I can't try to court someone whose husband has just died."

"But Papa, she's ready when you are." He narrowed his eyes at her.

"How do you know?"

"She talks about you all the time. It's been almost 2 months and she will need help with the children. You're not that much older than her, Papa. At least consider it."

The next night at dinner, there was a special announcement: Ms. Troyer and Mr. Miller were to begin courting, but slowly at first. Papa had decided that they could at least explore the possibility and the best way for that to happen was while they were in the same house together.

"I have a beautiful daughter that will keep me in check for the time being and a son who watches everything I do. I won't let you down." He smiled at Matthew and Rebecca.

The only thing left to do was see if Luke was still serious about courting. Rebecca had left him alone during the rebuilding of the community, but now that they were done and there was a new preacher in place, she knew this was the best time to talk to him.

She found him sitting at an old picnic table on the back side of the church. The weather had warmed up considerably and much of the snow that wasn't directly on the ground had melted. Rebecca joined him and decided to get right to it.

"Are we still going to court?" Luke was quiet for a while and Rebecca began to wonder if he had even heard her. She almost asked the question again until he answered.

"I think so."

"You think so?" He nodded.

"If we do this," they locked eyes, "this is it. I don't go around and 'try out' girls like some of the other guys do. It's either me, or it's the dating game." Rebecca wanted to answer quickly but realized that she needed to think about this. She was only 16 and if this was it, there would be no other. She stared at the table for a few minutes while she thought, but she knew her answer.

"This has always been it." She looked at him. "At the end of the day, it's always you and me, leading the way. We make sure our families are provided for and that everyone is safe. Why not do it together?"

"Wow," Luke said after a minute. "That was really poetic. Do you always talk like that?" Rebecca shrugged.

"I guess you bring the poet out in me."

"Either that, or I bring out a panic attack."

They laughed as Luke bent down and threw some snow in Rebecca's direction. This was truly the man she wanted to be with, and she knew that nothing else would be so important as this decision here and now. This beautiful friendship would turn into a beautiful romance... and that was the best thing for Rebecca and for her father. She was glad for this new stage in life and wanted nothing else than to enjoy this snowball fight with the man that would soon become her husband.

www.ingramcontent.com/pod-product-compliance
Lightning Source LLC
Chambersburg PA
CBHW021956170726

47994CB00021B/818